ABSOLUTION

Ólafur Jóhann Ólafsson

ABSOLUTION

A NOVEL

PANTHEON BOOKS NEW YORK

Library of Congress Cataloging-in-Publication Data

Ólafur Jóhann Ólafsson.
[Fyrirgefning syndanna. English]
Absolution: a novel/Ólafur Jóhann Ólafsson.
p.   cm.
ISBN 0-679-42891-7
I. Title.
PT7511.0439F9613 1994
839'.6934—dc20   93-41229

BOOK DESIGN BY M. KRISTEN BEARSE

Manufactured in the United States of America
First American Edition
9 8 7 6 5 4 3 2 1

ABSOLUTION

My sins will not be forgiven; I do not ask forgiveness and forgive nothing myself. I have nothing to lose; no one can take anything from me which has not already slipped my grasp. All is vanity, our clouded eyes see only a fragment of the vast picture; we say light is pleasant, it delights the eye to look at the sun, then we lean back in a soft chair with a cup of tea, waiting for sunset, knowing that nights will be long when summer is over.

There are few summers left now and my body, a reservoir of malignancies, keeps pace with my thoughts only intermittently. Today, however, my hand is strong; that is evident when I clench my fist and the knuckles whiten and my veins swell. I have no apprehensions about death, do not fear it, believing in nothing beyond it but emptiness. But I have much to complete before my farewell.

She will see that there still is life within me; she will marvel at my power and toughness, when I pry her knees apart and descend upon her. She will have no doubt that I am a match for anyone her age; she will admire my stamina and fear it at the same time. She will need to rest afterward, as I half-open the window, spread a sheet over her and let her sleep. When she awakens, she will radiate silent well-being, like meadowsweet after a shower of rain. She will search me out repeatedly, and I will pray for strength, pray for power for a few weeks more, a few days—a moment.

The road has always been stony and treacherous, its mansions full of labyrinths, its loneliness constant, its silence broken only by distant voices. You have heard much said about me, usually in whispers: a hand cupped between a mouth and an ear, evasive eyes, tense voices. You have heard stories in coffeehouses before the waiter brings the drinks (and everyone falls silent), at parties of the rich who have had to deal with me, in offices of corporations (including the one I founded myself), in conference rooms, in the lavatories of opera houses, on the streets, in taxicabs after the theater. You have heard stories, many stories, true and fictitious, about everything under the sun—everything except my little crime. Nobody but me knows about that.

Now that the affairs of the world have become a pantomime and pawns have seized power from kings and queens, it is easy for me to bid farewell and become dust like all the others. A patch of earth awaits me in the old Reykjavik cemetery, by my parents' side, a stone's throw from where I first caroused. There I shall return from the capitals of the world. I ask for nothing more than a moment's strength before I depart, to prove to her that I am not a decrepit old man, not a wretch with a walking stick and clouded eyes. One moment's power, and her knees will spread apart. All else I renounce: apples in a bowl, red wine, the smell of wet wool. Everything but closeness to her soft skin.

It would be a pleasure to watch them fighting over the inheritance, as soon as the lid shuts over my coffin. I imagine all of them in the study, before I am even cold in my grave: the children banding together at first to fight my second wife, because I know she will want more than I gave her in our divorce settlement. They are all greedy, despicable, trivial. Later the brother and sister will turn against each other, venomously, stopping at nothing to have their own way. Insults, backbiting, slander and treachery: these will be their instruments of torture. What a delight it would be to witness their conflicts, if only from afar. The arrangements I have contrived will make their misery long and bitter. I have done everything in my power to bring forth their inner nature, and may the Lord Almighty—in whom I do not believe—be my witness that it will be a nasty affair when they clash. They will not say of me, "His fruits are delicious to me."

It rained this morning. This evening it will grow colder. My hand is weary; I will put my pen down shortly.

Tonight she will buy takeout and we will eat supper without saying a word to each other in the kitchen. Later I will sit still in the darkness, in front of the television.

I do not sleep much anymore; the mill is falling silent, and the women too. I ask for only a moment's strength: I know that my sins will not be forgiven.

Oh, the dreams! Spare me from them; don't make me have to look at those images again; spare me the palpitations and the cold sweat. Give me a night of sleep without interruptive nightmares. Although I do not know you, do not believe in you . . . spare me!

I must have fallen asleep in front of the television. She had rented an old Laurence Olivier movie, and I sat down to watch it after supper. I enjoy old movies, even though I forget them as soon as they are over. I don't recall when I began to feel drowsy, nor when I awoke again, but I know for certain that I had no idea where I was. Sometimes, between sleeping and waking, I see myself standing alongside the actors in the movie, in black-and-white and looking as fit as they; we make plans together, console each other, drive through the city streets after a long night, looking for a place to have breakfast. I am invariably helpful to these people: I have twice saved Cary Grant's life, on more than one occasion have delved into my pocket for money to help Humphrey Bogart eat. And Greta Garbo, I know her well too. Ah, those soft lips. . . .

He's pathetic, you say. Senile and decrepit. But don't be so quick to judge me; allow me to continue before you pronounce your verdict.

Tonight I rescued no one and no one kissed me or

cuddled me. Tonight that nightmare haunted me again, its images clearer and more persistent than ever. (Oh, how clear they are!) I was running down a deserted street in the dark, my little crime behind me, no one in pursuit, no sound except the echo of my shoes against the cobbles. I turned a corner: royal photographs in dim shop windows. My little crime behind me, but still incomplete. The ship leaves at dawn. . . .

I woke up drenched in sweat, the video long since finished, white lines chasing each other down the screen. No mercy, I said to myself. How long must I endure this?

She was sleeping curled up at my feet, her black hair glittering, her breathing slow and rhythmic. I don't know why she has chosen to go on living here. She demands nothing, does not seem to be harboring any secret agenda, does not seem to be chasing after anything for herself. Obedient as a . . . no, I do not have permission to commit that to paper.

I stumbled into the bathroom, supported myself with both hands on the washbasin, took off my soaking shirt, splashed my face with water and waited for my heartbeat to calm down. Before I knew it, she was at my side with a damp flannel, stroking my back and chest, washing my armpits, running the flannel over my shoulders and stomach. Then she dried me and went off quietly to fetch a clean shirt, her movements lithe as a cat's.

In the green chair in the study I waited for morning. It was quiet outside, apart from the occasional ambulance on its way to Mount Sinai Hospital. I could not sleep, could neither read nor write. I stared at changes in the statues, the paintings and books all around me, as darkness yielded to the grayness of morning, creeping unassumingly between the curtains into the room. I began to feel better, for the nightmares are accustomed to vanish with the arrival of the morning light. I looked forward to breakfast: eggs, bread, cheese and a cup of coffee, perhaps at the old lady's place on the corner, perhaps at Manuel's on Seventy-second Street. I toyed at weighing the advantages against the disadvantages: Manuel bakes better bread than the old lady, but her place is quieter and there is more light to read the newspaper.

They will be surprised when they find the envelope in the bank vault and the papers at my lawyer's. He has been given strict orders not to waver from my instructions: to drag out distributing the inheritance and not show them all the documents at once, but make a long ordeal of it instead; hand one document over to them this week, another the next, make them think they have stumbled into paradise today, then tomorrow present them with the obligations that will reduce their wealth to nothing, drag everything out, move slowly, for patience is something they do not know, not even my daughter who became a devout Catholic at the request of her husband, that useless dandy.

"Father, I have sinned," she will whisper. "A whole month has passed since I visited you last, and much has happened to me since then. My thoughts are grim. I have betrayed my brother, done my utmost to beat him down, spoken badly of his wife and children, double-crossed him and felt hateful thoughts toward him. . . ."

"Forgive me, Father, for I have sinned. Four weeks have passed since I last visited you, weeks that our late father would have delighted in observing, were he still alive."

I decided to go to Manuel's for breakfast, longing to hear his chatter and the crackling of eggs frying in butter. I wanted to smell bacon and car exhausts through the window. I wanted to smell life.

When I go back home, I shall have the girl read the papers to me. The day is bright. Nothing will inconvenience me until dark.

*E*vents that will cause turmoil in our lives often seem so banal at first that later we cannot even remember them.

Around the time I received the manuscript, the West and East Germans had decided to reunite. Russia was holding Lithuania by the scruff of its neck, and a water pipe had burst in my kitchen. The telephone call I received one lazy afternoon from a lawyer friend, Herbert Schwartzman, seemed no more than yet another thread in the routine tapestry of my daily life.

I had started the day by translating into French a letter from my boss to his Belgian agent. I had been striving to find words in the tongue of Rolland and Baudelaire that best captured his alarm and disappointment at the poor sales of biscuits, canned foods and tobacco across the whole of Europe—but in particular Belgium. Since there are no windows in my part of the office, I had gotten up and strolled down the corridor to watch the spring rain as I mulled over a handful of words that needed to be improved in my translation. I do not recall how I had been feeling that day; I guess I did not feel any different from most other days since she left, neither better nor worse. Anyway, I stood a while watching the rain pouring over the yellow taxicabs on the street below and the people who rushed into them or darted out in search of other shelter. I told myself that with luck it would stop raining before I finished work. When I slunk back to my desk, the telephone rang.

"I've been working on the estate of a compatriot of yours,"

Herbert Schwartzman said when we had finished exchanging pleasantries. "I don't know whether you've ever heard of him. Peter Peterson was his name. Filthy rich but one hell of an eccentric."

I had not heard of this Peter Peterson—or Pétur Pétursson, as his original name must presumably have been—and I was surprised, since I thought I knew about most other Icelanders in this city, if not all of them, having either met them at social functions or at least heard of them through the grapevine.

Schwartzman doubted whether I could have met Peter Peterson socially. "Hardly ever left his house in his last years," he said. "But maybe you can still help me. We found a manuscript with some of his things in a locked vault in his house; his children think it's in Icelandic, but neither of them knows the language.

"It may or may not be of significance. I told them I know someone who can read it swiftly. You know the way we lawyers are trained to think. God is in the details."

I said I would gladly do him this favor, and we arranged to meet the following day at a nearby restaurant, where he handed me the manuscript in a brown envelope.

The bulky manuscript seemed a random heap of papers. I started reading it later that evening and did not put it down until dawn. By then my nerves were taut, and I could not get to sleep no matter how I tried.

I was on edge most of the following day, had trouble concentrating on the most trivial of tasks, could not even work on letters from my boss to his agents in Germany, Switzerland and Spain, even though they were essentially no different from the one sent off two days earlier. I called Schwartzman to say that the manuscript consisted of nothing more than the incoherent memoirs of an old man. But I left work early and walked up Park Avenue until I reached Peter Peterson's address, haunted by what I had read. I *stood for a while across the street, watching people leave the building and cars stop in front, until the thought occurred to me how close inquisitiveness is to prying.*

When I returned home that evening, I began, as if by instinct, to translate the manuscript. I became so obsessed with it that I found myself revising, amending and abridging it as if I were its original author. For the next few months I spent evenings this way, sitting at the desk that she and I had bought in a little town where the Hudson River is at its widest and the boats slow down to allow their passengers a splendid view. Then everything was still fine between us.

As I approach the end of this task I set for myself, I am still no nearer to understanding why I undertook it, unrequested, unauthorized. I have not changed the tone of the original, though I have tried to harmonize the account as best I could. Sometimes I feel that Peterson's words might just as easily have flowed from my own pen.

I have walked the streets he describes in his writings, eaten at the restaurants he frequented. I have even spoken to the doorman in the building where he lived, feeling almost as if I were he. I have had to reprimand myself, warn myself not to overstep my bounds when entertaining the notion of contacting his son or the girl who lived with him.

Now the summer is drawing to a close and the last heat wave is passing over the city. The air is humid and my body feels clammy at night. People lie awake in the night and by day take things slowly, bow their heads. The occasional cabdriver can be heard whistling snatches of a tune. Myself, I go to a coffeehouse down the street after work and ask for a sidewalk table, because my apartment feels empty and I don't like the prospect of going back to it.

I gesture to the waiter to bring me a sandwich and another glass of wine. God willing, the afternoon sun might manage to shine through the haze.

The years of childhood—it is always thought appropriate to mention them.

I was brought up in a middle-class home in Reykjavik. My childhood passed without any major interventions on the part of Providence, for God created everything in the interests of middle-class homes in the capital. Our house stood at the foot of the Holavalla hill. A father taking his young son for a walk around the lake on a bright winter morning would have seen its red roof and white window frames on the other side in the cold tranquility of the morning; he might also have noticed that the ground-floor curtains were open. There were vases of dried flowers in the windows, but this could not be seen from the other side of the lake. On the upper floor, the curtains in the north window would in all probability have been drawn, because I tended to sleep in the morning and used to enjoy lying in bed until the maid, on my mother's orders, would force me to get up. In the winter, blue curtains would be hung in my room, bright ones with golden embroidery in the summer. Nothing disturbed my sleep, and my dreams were harmless, unmemorable when I awoke.

• • •

When I get up I put on the boxing gloves that my father gave me as a birthday present last week. I stretch out my arms and clench my fists, put one foot forward and bend my knees, like boxers in magazines. Then I take on imaginary adversaries, delivering one blow after another until they slump to the ground. Myself, I escape with only a few scratches. I put on my baggy pants and sweater, drink hot cocoa in the kitchen and watch the snow on the branches of the trees in the garden while the maid hums the latest hits from Denmark. It must have snowed all night. In the afternoon, my friends and I will go tobogganing on the hill. A church is being built to the greater glory of God on the meadow there.

In the evening my family sits in the drawing room, playing cards or solitaire. I play with tin soldiers on the floor.

At nine o'clock I am told to go to bed, while my older sister is allowed to stay up half an hour later (in fact, I suspect this half hour will be extended to a full hour). Then Mother sits down with embroidery in the corner chair by the window, and Father reads a book or browses through the latest magazines, like *Angler* and *Popular Mechanics*, lights his pipe and allows the smoke to merge with the tranquility of the room. Later he will go down to the little room in the basement to knit fishing flies or work with a plane, saw or hammer. I like the smell of wood and tobacco. Father never looks tired after his day's work, for his business runs itself: everyone needs drapes and clothing and there is little competition. He never talks about business at home; he never mentions money or tells stories about his staff or customers unless Mother asks him. He always wears dark or gray suits and a white shirt, with either a necktie or a bow tie. His methodical manner aside, he is a cheerful man, with the playful streak typical of people from his part of the country. My paternal grandfather was a fisherman-farmer from north Iceland. My mother, however, is Danish, a merchant's daughter and not exactly an authority on human misery and poverty.

On warm summer days they sit at a round table in the garden and drink tea with their friends or neighbors.

It is Friday. I know because I have been counting days since Tuesday when I took to bed with the flu. Frissi came by day before yesterday, but my mother would not let him in, saying I might pass the disease on to him. I repeated the Lord's Prayer three times this morning and seven times yesterday, adding a prayer for quick recovery and promising in return better behavior, yet I still have not noticed any results. I put down my Tarzan comic for the hundredth time; I know it by heart.

After lunch my mother visits a friend. They play bridge on Fridays. My sister Disa is not due back from school until three. I keep thinking about Frissi; he must have gone to play football with the boys on the meadow after school. I hope Ferdinand, the head gardener, doesn't see them. Although it has not rained since yesterday, the meadow is probably still wet.

"Don't go running around without getting dressed properly, my boy," my father told me this morning. "The flu will get worse."

"Unless you want to be sick for three weeks again like last year," added Disa unnecessarily.

I am bored with faking coughing fits and calling for the maid so that I can hear her running furiously up the stairs; she does not even speak Icelandic. She is Norwegian or

Danish, I don't remember which. I hope Mother will buy me a new Tarzan comic on her way home.

The wind has died down outside, has ceased howling in the eaves. After lunch I hear the maid tidying up in the kitchen. Now everything is quiet. But suddenly I become aware of a rustling downstairs. I think I hear my father in the house. Disobeying his instructions, I get out of bed and put on my slippers and dressing gown. I sneak down the stairs, moving slowly because I'm a little dizzy. I still have a fever—so much for the power of prayer. Everything seems normal on my way down: the bell rope in the hallway and the flowerpot on the landing. I have often bumped into that flowerpot when I was rushing down the stairs.

At first the study door looks shut, but as I draw closer, I can see inside. On the settee where Father often naps, the maid is lying with her skirt hitched up and her legs apart. Father is standing over her, taking his time about it, patiently unbuttoning his fly, undoing his suspenders, dropping his underpants. He lies on top of her.

"Herr Finsen!" she exclaims (she always calls him Herr Finsen, despite my repeated attempts to correct her). "Oh, Herr Finsen!"

He does what he's doing in the same way as everything else he undertakes: confidently, with a steadfast air of authority. Without agitation, without fumbling, without pausing to review his work in progress. I watch his backside rising and falling, his necktie dangling in her face as she tries to brush it aside. "Finsen, oh, Herr Finsen. . . ." The pendulum of the dining-room clock swings to and fro like the Almighty's baton conducting time and silence and my father's undulations on the settee. The springs creak pleasantly, and the rhythm is in no way incongruous with the calm inside the house. Father's backside is breaking out in a sweat as he labors; the maid has stopped calling Father Herr Finsen, and the only sounds she makes are gentle groans. Then, she becomes quiet. Father lies still for a moment, before rising to his feet and pulling up his pants.

I rush back up to bed, hoping that my disobedience has not worsened my condition. I wonder if Mother will buy me a new Tarzan comic on her way home.

G ot a cigarette?"
 "No," I replied.

"Shit. I didn't realize I'd finished the pack already."

We were standing against the southern wall of the high school, having just come out of English class for recess. Frissi tapped his knuckles against the wall, straightened his tie and brushed invisible lint from his jacket.

"I can't believe we don't have any cigarettes left."

Spring, cold air but bright sky; calm, and the mountain there as usual, on the other side of the bay, companion of generations.

"Let's go play billiards," Frissi suggested.

"We don't have time."

"We have fifteen minutes. Let's get some cigarettes at least."

We went down to the square; the billiard hall was down by the harbor. Wearing the new jacket my mother had ordered from Germany, I adapted my gait to show it off. I was convinced that passersby were noticing the way I was dressed.

The billiard hall was dim; clouds of smoke were everywhere; the lights were low. Men of various ages were wielding their cues in silence, leaning over the table with one eye closed; cigarettes dangling from their lips, glowing and darkening by turns. We greeted some of the regulars we knew and set up a rack on a table in the corner. Two classmates of ours were in the middle of a game in the far corner.

"Snooker?"

"Alright, but we'll have to make it quick."

We had begun to frequent the place the previous fall, Frissi first, then the rest of us. Sometimes during recess, sometimes after school. We played for money, but never for a lot: one krona at the most.

"We'll be taking finals before we know it."

"Winter came and went in a hurry, didn't it?"

"Yeah."

"Funny how time flies."

We took our time, even though we should have been back in school by now. Our high school years drawing to a close, graduation ahead and long days after. Frissi was in good form: I had the feeling he might even win half a krona off me.

"What are you going to do in the fall, Frissi?"

"I don't know."

"Why aren't you going to university?"

"I'm bored by school. It's time I started making some money."

Few people left in the billiard hall, our classmates gone off to their lessons, clerks back behind their desks. A cab-driver I recognized was playing with the owner of the place at a table by the front door.

"We can't all go off to Denmark like you," Frissi said. "We're not big intellectuals like you."

"But you've always done better than me at school."

Frissi put down his cue, lit another cigarette and leaned against the windowsill.

"My dad can't afford to send me to Copenhagen. You might not have heard, but there's a depression going on around here. And anyway, I can't be bothered hanging around school anymore. My ass gets sore when I sit on it all day."

"But don't you think it's worth going to university? Don't you think you're missing out on. . . ."

"Pete, Pete," he interrupted me. "Why are you so naive sometimes?"

He cleared the table; I handed over a krona. Jingling the coins in his palm, he grinned. "Maybe I'll be able to afford college after all."

It was afternoon when we crossed the square, heading south down Laekjargata. Frissi suggested we go look in some windows along the Austurstraeti before going back to school, but I didn't think so; there was no telling whether my father might see us and demand an explanation for my absence from school. I rarely missed a class, but this time I didn't feel any remorse.

We sat down on a stone fence where we wouldn't be seen from the school and lit some more cigarettes, since there were still ten minutes left until the next class started.

"Funny how time flies. So you're off to Denmark in the fall."

"It's something to do."

"I can't believe you're chasing her all the way to Denmark. Do you really think she'll go for you any more in Denmark than she did here?"

"What are you talking about?"

"Gudrún. It didn't take you long to decide what to do when you heard she was going to Copenhagen in the fall."

I didn't reply.

"Why on earth are you chasing her? She's been leading you on for over a year. Playing games with you. You're still not any closer. Movies. A couple of dances. Walks around the lake. A peck on the cheek. And you're chasing her all the way to Copenhagen!"

Class time. We stamped out our cigarettes on the sidewalk.

"I don't understand you."

"Cut it out, Frissi."

"I just don't understand you."

On our way back over to the school building, I was surprised to find a billiard ball in my jacket pocket. I stopped and began to toss it from hand to hand.

"Did you steal a billiard ball, asshole?"

"I've no idea how it got there. I've no idea . . . I've got to take it back."

"Take it back? What are you going to say? 'Excuse me, Mr. Sivertsen, but I stole your ball. Sorry. I didn't mean to.' You'd be better off swallowing the fucking thing than giving it back."

He smirked. I could not trust him. But worse, I could not trust myself either.

I put the ball back in my pocket and watched the black coal smoke rising from the chimneys.

How you twisted me around your finger. How you forced me to chase you all over the place, dream about you at night, anticipate seeing you by day. How you humored my immaturity by gently stroking my cheek after the movies, when shyly I confessed my love. You were stunning, there is no denying that. Your dark brown hair soft as silk, your teeth sparkling white, your eyes like pearls in clear water. Your movements kindled a yearning in my body that I had never known before. There was something about you that drew our female classmates to you; you were the leader of the pack, they followed every example you set. The plainer ones swarmed around you like bees around their queen; others envied you, but followed you all the same. You could inflict wounds with silence, the suggestion of a smile or sardonic glance. You were invariably smartly dressed, because your father always bought you new clothes whenever he went abroad. You were never loud, never imposing. You never had to be.

I have often wondered why you bothered to waste your time with me. I was such easy prey, such a sure catch. Maybe I encouraged your vanity: I lived in a big house in the quarter where the Reykjavik gentry lived; my father was a well-known businessman, my mother a respected woman. But as for me, I was nothing more than an awkward kid, barely average in height, plump, sensitive, certainly no leader. I withered at sarcasm, lost my temper easily and cried like a baby when I felt I was being taken advantage of. My attempts at being funny somehow always turned out to be at someone else's expense; from an early age I had had a knack for spotting other people's weaknesses. I had a hard time figuring out girls my age. If I tried to draw attention to myself, I always ended up falling flat on my face. You, on the other hand, immediately gained a hold over me and knew I had to obey you like a humble servant.

Do you remember the first time I proposed to you? It was outdoors, in the Pavilion Gardens, late autumn, well into the evening. A flock of swans were flying westward. Of course, you were right when you said we were much too young.

"Not now," you said. "We'll talk about that later. There's plenty of time."

You managed to humiliate me without letting me actually lose hope. She's right, I would tell myself . . . she doesn't want to rush into anything . . . yet she did not refuse, just postponed our agreeing on the time and place. After all, there is plenty of time. . . .

How could *he* have escaped my notice? It is incomprehensible to me. I did not know about him until I had been in Denmark for over a month. How you managed to keep your relationship with him secret still remains a mystery to me. You were cunning. Cunning and scheming. Did he know about me? It doesn't matter anyway; there was nothing to know about. You treated me like a child.

When was it that you started to go with him? The year we graduated—or earlier? You were clever enough not to choose one of our classmates to torture me, for that would have been too easy. I would have found out sooner or later. When did you start the game? Did you always intend to humiliate me? Right from the start, the first time I asked you out to see *Gone With the Wind*? Were you thinking about him as we sat in the darkness, while you took my hand and stroked the palm? Were you thinking about him as I took courage and put my arm around you? Were you thinking about him the whole time?

"I'm going to Copenhagen this fall to work as an au pair. They're people my father knows. The husband runs a textile factory. They have three children. The youngest is three, the others just into their teens. I want to see the world. I want to get to know different countries, learn Danish better, grow up. . . . I'll only be gone a year. A year will be over before you know it, Pete."

Can you imagine how I felt when you told me? Can you understand my misery in the days that followed? Then my joy when Father agreed to send me to Copenhagen after I nagged him for days and weeks on end? How innocent of me, what an appalling fool I was.

Father was misty-eyed when I said goodbye at the harbor. Mother patted me on the shoulder and told me I was a man now.

"Write as often as you can," Mother said.

I fought back tears, tried not to show emotion.

"Be careful," Father said.

At sea, people are neither as they were at home nor as they will be at the end of the journey. The mind is altered. Those waving goodbye from a ship are transformed the moment they vanish from sight.

P lease, can you spare a dollar? Anything. How about a quarter? A quarter, man.

"Hey, that sandwich you're carrying, are you gonna eat it all yourself? It's a sandwich, ain't it? Come on . . . give me a piece; I haven't eaten anything in two days."

I quickened my pace, rushed away from him, my heart racing, my legs heavy. He chased me, this scum, his clothes torn and dirty, his stench appalling. He was holding out a red paper cup at me, shaking it, small change clinking in it. Unable to endure his stench and his persistence, I quickened my pace even faster. He stopped, but his gaze followed me. I could feel him on the nape of my neck, my back, my legs.

Out of his sight around the corner, I slowed down and wiped sweat from my brow. Realizing I had been gripping the sandwich bag tightly with one hand and the change in my overcoat pocket with the other, I relaxed and threw the sandwich into the garbage bin. I had lost my appetite for it. They are everywhere, these scum: in every alleyway, on every corner, in the subway, at restaurant entrances. Everywhere. Junkies, layabouts, thugs and crooks.

I hardly dare leave the building anymore, never go anywhere alone except to the old woman's or Manuel's to eat fried eggs with a little bacon. Everywhere else I go by cab.

I always look around when I go out onto the street, ask the doorman if it's all clear. "Yes, Mr. Peterson," he answers. "All clear. Everything is just fine. The lady on the fifth floor is in the hospital."

He has been working in the building for years and I am beginning to trust him a little. He does not seem to be either a thief or a busybody, always follows my orders and tells people who come in off the street wanting to visit me that I am not in. That is why my daughter dislikes him so much. I remember once she pushed her way past him, strutted through the lobby and into the elevator. He phoned me immediately and warned me of her arrival. I made sure the doors were locked. She stood out there for at least fifteen minutes, ringing the bell and rattling the doorknob, before she calmed down and began to weep. When I sneaked a peek through the peephole, I could see her face bloated with tears and impudence. She was not in the least different from when she was a child, except that now she did not stamp her feet, having realized that this kind of behavior produces scant results. I waited for her to leave, watching her face and movements to try to understand better what her problem was. As usual, she reminded me of her mother; no wonder they get on so well together and often meet to disparage me. But I need not worry about her mother: she got her fair share when we divorced and cannot make any further claims. I came through the divorce reasonably well, armed as I was with some information about her lawyer that he would have regretted to hear in public. All the same, I was fair, that cannot be denied, and by no means treated her dishonorably. But that is another story.

My son has started to realize that I do not care for visits from him either, so he does not come by anymore. Besides, he lacks initiative and is soft in character. A weakling, I must say. His sister pushes him around.

Not long ago my daughter bumped into the girl when she went out to buy some food and rent a video. I suspect my daughter waited in ambush: she did not accompany the girl into the food store, but waited for her outside. My daughter was sycophantic at first, then brash, and finally rude when the girl would not answer her questions.

"How is he feeling? Does he visit the doctor regularly? Is he taking his medication?"

Then: "How does he spend his time? Is he still fiddling about with business and finance? Does he ever talk about me? What does he say? Surely he must say something?"

Finally: "It's obvious he's taking advantage of you. What exactly do you do for him? You ought to be ashamed of yourself! Probably stealing from him too. . . . Don't give me this attitude, you slut! Don't think you can get away with it! And don't be stupid enough to imagine you can get money out of him. It belongs to the family. Watch your step. . . ."

Tough as the girl is, she must have been affected by all this. She did not complain when she came in; I had to follow her into the kitchen and drag the story out of her. She told it without working herself up while arranging cans in the pantry. She was completely calm, her movements lithe as a cat's. I once asked her whether they eat cats in Cambodia. She did not reply.

Sometimes she sleeps badly. She does not toss and turn (she always sleeps in a fetal position), but she emits the sounds of a wounded animal, neither loud nor shrill. It's enough to wake me up; she must be in great pain.

In the evening we ate liver after having some canned tuna with onion. I went into my wine cellar and chose a good bottle of red (I know my son covets my collection of wines, especially my vintage Bordeaux), poured it into a carafe and allowed it to breathe before tasting it. It was as if I were releasing a spirit from the bottle when I pulled the cork, allowing it to come into being and adjust to its new environment.

I sipped the wine slowly, imagining a long, hot summer, fresh fruit, sunshine and billowing white skirts; honey and roses, a breeze and footsteps in the garden. I finished the bottle with my mind numbed; I had a hunch I would soon be falling into a deep sleep. I hoped my night would be dreamless.

Forgive me, Father, for I have sinned. It has been a long time since I entered your house; your voice is unfamiliar to me and your image too. I have heard you mentioned, of course, but I do not believe in you. Beyond life, nothing awaits us: the lights of our eyes go out; the body stiffens. But I have heard people talk about you, as you can well imagine.

Father, some of my recent dreams have been bizarre. I do not understand them. And I am not referring to my recurring nightmare, but to other dreams. I dreamed last night that I was making love to my maternal aunt Martha. How can any man dream such a thing? What would make him do so? What in me gives rise to such dreams? I am half-frightened by them—as I am by many other things I do not understand.

I last thought about Aunt Martha decades ago. I do not recall ever desiring her, do not recall anything of that sort ever crossing my mind. After all, she was Mother's sister! Eighteen years younger than Mother, admittedly, but her sister all the same. In the dream I was an old man. Perhaps ten years younger than I am now. She, however, was the way I remember her best: a young woman in her early thirties. It is to my credit, though, that I dreamt of her as being younger than she would be now. Or is it? Does that actually make a difference?

The dream was long and detailed. And Aunt Martha was whispering words in my ear that I am convinced she would never have let herself be heard saying in her lifetime. I can reasonably assume she never even heard these words spoken. What could possibly be the reason I dreamed about her in this way? Of course, I have no control over what I dream, any more than anybody else, but there is still no one to blame but myself. If I believed in you, the obvious thing would be to blame you for these dreams. But since I do not believe in you, I shall refrain from doing so.

There is not much justice in this world. And it is difficult to distinguish between the injustice of men and your justice. Whenever I think of my aunt Martha from now on, the dream will be part of that memory. Even though I know that it has no foundation in conventional reality. I remember words she did not say and events that never took place. Is that not peculiar?

Let us conjecture that I might tell someone who knew Martha about this dream. Her son, for instance. Would the account of my dream inevitably be preserved somewhere in his brain? Might it not possibly also change his memory of his mother? Even if I were to make it perfectly clear that this was nothing more than fantasy. I could, in other words, turn other people's memories of my aunt upside down merely by recounting the nonsensical dream of an old man. One person tells another—and everything is changed.

This is not to imply that it would ever enter my mind to mention this to anybody at all. Far from it. I am only toying with this conceit in order to demonstrate to myself and others the powers of illusion. Delusion, lies, plots, treachery: they shape our lives and we cannot do a thing about it. And we bid this world farewell hardly knowing what was true and what was false.

Father, the reason I take the liberty of addressing you on these scraps of paper, even though I do not believe in you and even though the God-fearing are convinced that our paths will never cross, is in fact very simple: it is Sunday morning, and my thoughts turned to you when I sat down at my desk and heard the church bells chiming in the distance. I opened the window, because the sound was pleasant and the air was clear after last night's rain. Then an old Latin phrase that I once memorized for an examination, and for some reason has never left my brain, began to echo. *Quam salubre est sedere in solitudine et loqui cum Deo*— How cleansing it is to sit in solitude and speak with God.

Salubre, I said to myself, sat down at the desk and decided to address you in a short note about my aunt Martha and delusion in the world.

Salubre.

Before proceeding any further, I want to refresh my own memory about how the girl happened to move into my house. I know this is a digression; according to the rules, I should doubtless be describing something else. But since I and nobody else decides, I will do what I please.

Just over three years ago (three years and four months, to be precise) I fell ill. That was six months after I had divorced my second wife, but my illness was in no way connected to the divorce, which was more an occasion of joy than of sadness to me. Anyway, I fell ill. And doctors of varying degrees of wisdom—some of them such boys that there was nothing on their faces for them to shave—unanimously pronounced a quick death sentence: "Mr. Peterson, it looks bad. Your heart is useless—completely useless, to tell the truth—and there's nothing we can do. Really, it's amazing that you've hung on as long as you have. Six, seven months more: you should be thankful for every week after that. . . ."

They strictly forbade me to continue to work, sent me home in a cab because I was not allowed to walk, not allowed to overexert myself, and made me swallow pills for breakfast, lunch and dinner. The drugs ran me down: I suffered insomnia, was exhausted during the day, incapable of doing anything constructive, my mind empty. My children and ex-wives feigned all manner of worry, because they could all smell money and thought this was their last chance to ingratiate themselves with me.

The day my death sentence was pronounced, I disobeyed my doctors and took a cab and instructed the driver to drive around instead of hurrying home to hibernate in bed. It was cold, the middle of February, and windy to boot. We drove around that part of town where my office had been for almost forty years. I stared at the houses and garages, restaurants and stores, preparing for the fact that this might be the last time I would see them. We drove aimlessly like this for a half hour, an hour, before I went into the office and told John Lazarus, my partner and companion for half a century, that I would be going away for some time. At first he did not believe me, but when he realized I was not joking, I noticed that the news had a deep impact on him.

"Let's keep this between you and me," I said. "No need to let the staff or customers know."

He naturally agreed to everything I proposed (no one argues with a condemned man) and asked me time and again if there was anything he could do for me: "Anything, just name it, anything. . . ." He was a fine fellow, bless his soul, and always took my advice, was always ready to put in a hard day's work, even though he was perhaps only of average intelligence. Bless his soul again. Now that he is dead, I have to deal with his idiot son, whom nobody remembered to raise properly.

I hired a private nurse and lay at home in a stupor for four months, until early in June when I decided I would prefer to die in my right mind after a week than to lie like a zombie for a few extra months. I fired the nurse, thanked her for her pleasant company, tossed my drugs into the toilet. It took me only three days to recover my power and energy. I began eating eggs for breakfast again—what a pleasure, the smell of fried bacon and fresh coffee—drank red wine in the evenings, strolled the streets when I pleased, felt my body and soul rising from the ashes. On the seventh day, however, I did not rest but decided to make a quick trip to the office to make sure everything was in order and that no petty potentates were trying to stake their claims to the realm, no pawns were beginning to think they were kings. John, my partner, admittedly looked pleased to see me, but his worries outweighed his joy.

"What are you doing on your feet? You're supposed to be lying in bed and taking it easy. . . . You've stopped taking the drugs? Are you out of your mind? And you've sent the nurse away? You're crazy."

"She was useless," I said. "Flat as a pancake. No ass, and tits to match."

"You sound like you're feeling better," he said.

Nonetheless, he continued to niggle, asking me to take care, not rush into anything, not overexert myself, take life easy, enjoy the fine weather before it got humid and the heat became intolerable. Told me not to worry about the business, everything was going its old smooth way.

"The important thing is for you to get better," he said. "Enjoy the summer. Go out and pick up a woman. Smell the blossoms on the trees. Allow yourself to get well."

And since I was still feeling well after getting rid of the drugs and had no particular interest in spending the whole day sitting in my office once more, I agreed to take it easy for the next few weeks, work at home and—as he put it— enjoy life. Because maybe I had only a couple of weeks left.

The woman who had been my secretary for eighteen years had retired around the time of my illness, and I had had awful trouble finding a replacement. She had retired on her sixtieth birthday the previous fall and I had tried out many others since then, but none fit the bill. It's tough to find a good secretary in this city: some of them pretend to be actresses waiting for a role, or models, or authors, even though they are incapable of stringing together a simple business letter. While I was lying in my stupor, John's secretary had filled in and handled the work that needed to be done. Now, however, I was hard-pressed to find a secretary who could work both in the office and at my home.

"A young woman's been temping here recently," said John. "Oriental. Admittedly, she doesn't speak the language perfectly, but she's conscientious and a hard worker."

"I'll give her a try," I said. "Send her to my house at eleven tomorrow morning."

"Don't you want to speak to her first?"

I told John that I trusted him and would leave it to his discretion. "Maybe I should ask you to choose my next wife for me. So far I haven't been too successful myself."

The girl arrived punctually and has not left since. As it happened, she did not move in until later, but it feels as if she has always been here. Although I know nothing about her family, it seems unlikely that she is close to anyone else. She does not mention her past; I do not ask her about it. This is the best arrangement: no past, no future, only today.

Even though my cardiac disorder did not prove to be anything more than a misdiagnosed congenital defect, harmless and purely decorative, I did not return to work full-time at the office. At first I went three afternoons a week (Mondays, Wednesdays and Fridays), but since John died, all I have done is pop my head in occasionally. I cannot stand his son and have arranged things so as to give him little control. I appointed an outsider to run the company; my lawyers and financial advisers make sure he does not embark on any wild schemes. So far, he has put in a creditable performance.

The girl is loyal and obedient as a . . . no, I cannot allow myself to commit that to paper. She buys the food and pays the bills, goes to the bank and takes out money (I have long since given up keeping track of my day-to-day finances, since I know I can trust her), she cooks, cleans and keeps me company. She says little and smiles only rarely, but her hair is jet black and soft as silk. She asks no questions when I wake up from my nightmare in the middle of the night, drenched in sweat and groaning; she wipes me with a damp cloth and brings me a clean shirt. Give me strength, I say, give me power if only for an instant, and I shall show her that I am not an aging invalid. Her knees will move hesitantly apart and I will merge with her. Whisper in my ear what I alone may hear. Whisper it . . . a moment's power and I shall . . .

Tonight we will watch *Mr. Smith Goes to Washington*. She is beginning to tell Cary Grant and James Stewart apart, no longer confuses Bette Davis and Katharine Hepburn. She will sit at my feet; we will turn the lights down and I will run my fingers through her hair. It will be quiet outside, a half-moon in the eastern sky and street people rummaging through the trash cans at the back of the building. Perhaps they will find a bite to eat. I shall stroke a weary hand across her cheek, and for an instant my life will seem nothing but uninterrupted ecstasy.

It has been exactly three weeks since I returned home; yesterday it was two weeks and six days. Tomorrow it will be three weeks and a day. I know, because I have been counting the days, the minutes, the weeks, mornings, nights and strokes of the drawing-room clock. It was Monday yesterday. Now it is Tuesday. Squalls are raging outside, tugging at the naked branches of the trees.

I sleep badly at night. During the day I sit downstairs in the drawing room, smoking. There was all manner of weather at sea on the way home; but I remained sick whether it was stormy or calm, vomiting at regular intervals. Toward the end of the journey, I was throwing up only bile. I was drained when we arrived, and spent the first few days and nights lying in bed; my forehead hot, my body cold as my bones shivered.

"He's changed," I heard Father say.

"Grown up," said Mother.

They did not ask many questions at first but left me to rest in peace, sensing I was not ready to take part in long conversations. I got up late: instead of putting on my clothes, I would don a dressing gown and sit down with the newspaper and a cigarette in the kitchen to begin with, and then later in the drawing room. They disapproved of my smoking but did not say anything. For the first few days

Mother waited for me to get up in the morning so that she could make breakfast for both of us: boiled eggs, jam and cheese on toast, a pot of cocoa; but when I did not touch the food, when I simply asked the maid for coffee, she stopped, left me alone.

My parents went about their lives as usual, rigidly sticking to their routine even though the ship's arrival was considered major news in town, and my precarious health and changed personality caused both of them concern. Father would go off to work in the mornings; Mother would meet her friends according to accepted custom. Neither of them ever entertained the idea of postponing the dinner parties they had planned before I came home.

"He's never had a strong constitution," Mother told Mrs. Thorstensen while the maid was helping her take off her coat one day. "He still hasn't gotten over the sea voyage. Or the war and all that business in Denmark. He's absolutely exhausted."

"The partisanship," Father added. "Pétur has always been sensitive."

The chatter of the guests wafted up to my room; their laughter, the clanking of their cutlery and the smell of cigars kept me company while they were eating.

"What," said Father, "what . . . a lad his age doesn't want to read about business, he wants to do business. And I don't blame him either. Look at me, I've never read a word about business. It's in the blood. Anyone can learn bookkeeping, but only a handful of people have business in their blood."

"He wants to go to America," Mother said.

"That's where the prospects are," Father said. "He has

been offered a job as purchasing manager with Franklin & Svensen. Old Björn Svensen was delighted that Pétur wanted to take the job. Now he's just waiting for the next westbound ship."

"I don't like the sound of it," Mother said.

"What a thing to say," Father said. "What a thing to say. . . ."

They played bridge after the meal, the men drinking cognac and the women sherry.

"Four hearts," Mother called.

Mrs. Thorstensen redoubled. I went downstairs and into the kitchen without letting myself be seen, poured a glass of cognac and took it up to my room. The wind had died down as the evening wore on, and when I opened the window, I thought I could discern the first signs of winter in the air.

I lit a cigarette, sipped my cognac and thought about her, as I had every day since I left. I could see her there, in the room I had been renting: the book-lined shelves behind her as she sat looking out the window, two pictures on the wall above the desk, one of Mother and Father, the other of her.

I could see her sitting on the settee where I slept: "Pete, I must go. They're expecting me at eleven o'clock. You know how grouchy the old man gets."

I had heard that before, but now I know where you went when you said goodbye. I followed you across Fruentorg and into Skinnegade, without worrying that you would notice me, because you suspected nothing. You walked quickly; you were in a hurry to see him. I watched you disappear into the house where he lived, and I stood outside on the sidewalk until the light in his window went out and dew appeared on the street. Then I went home, looking for the new moon through the fog.

My parents' guests left around midnight. The maid is finishing washing up and wiping the tables in the drawing room. Then she will go to bed. I count the days until I leave for America.

Tomorrow: another newspaper and a fresh pack of cigarettes. Gray sky, cold earth.

I was not thinking about Iceland's mountains or its valleys when we left port and sailed for Scotland to meet the convoy, nor about the heather or the lakes, the trees in the old cemetery or dawn by the lakeside in Reykjavik. I did not know then how long it would be before I would return to Iceland, and even if I had known, I doubt whether my thoughts would have been any loftier.

Father and Mother saw me off at the harbor, but their embraces were different from those they had given me when I sailed for Denmark the previous year. There was melancholy warmth, uncertainty in Mother's eyes, as if she was not exactly sure of her son anymore.

"May God look after you, Pétur dear. It's a dangerous journey."

"You'll come through with flying colors," Father said. "Send us a telegram as soon as you reach America."

Mountains and spits, glaciers, headlands and peninsulas turned into a dark line between the sky and the ocean; the gulls vanished, the vastness of the sea was all. Eventually, the line grew lighter, merged with the endless grayness— became nothing. I was feeling rather fragile after going out to a dance with Frissi the night before, so I lay down in my bunk bed and tried to adjust to the roll of the ship. There were about a dozen passengers on board. I knew none of them.

I was not apprehensive about the journey, even though I was aware of its risk: German submarine warfare against convoys sailing between Europe and the U.S. I was at ease not only on the way to Scotland but also after we joined the convoy and sailed west. My little crime was behind me: nothing could be done to change what had happened. Perhaps there was no desire on my part to change anything.

I had been told there were at least twenty ships in front of us and fourteen or fifteen behind us. By day it was quiet, but at night there was fear of surprise attacks. The day before, German U-boats had sunk two ships in our convoy. Twenty ships in front of us, twelve or thirteen behind us now. On board, we all tried to raise each other's spirits by saying that the *Godafoss* was too small to interest the Germans. My bottle of cognac was empty; it was time to open my suitcase and find another, together with the pipe I had bought, already broken in, from Frissi.

While we were in Scotland over Christmas waiting to continue our journey, I got to know the other passengers better: a girl on her way to university, half a dozen males between twenty and fifty in search of opportunity and riches, a married couple with two children whom we called the Torfasons. I played whist with the daughter when I was in a good mood, and poker with the lads in the evening. We played for money and cigarettes; sometimes I was allowed to settle my debts with swigs of cognac. I broke even, but everyone else ended up in the red. That is to say everyone except Hannes Franzson, a man of thirty on the same mission as myself. He had a pallid complexion and kept his left hand in his jacket pocket, an unassuming character. Sometimes he gave the impression of knowing something the rest of us had no clue about. I didn't know what to make of him. He had left his wife and young daughter behind in Iceland. Hannes knew how to make money, there was no question about that. Hannes swept the tables.

"It's consoling to know your money is in my pocket, if they sink us. A consolation in such a tragedy. . . . "

"Deal, you bastard."

"Are you in, Pétur?"

"I'm in."

A rumbling in the distance. We fell silent for a while, then continued while calm was restored.

"A mine. They're really pumping them out tonight. What sort of hand do you think Hannes got?"

"He must be cheating."

"Out with your queen, Hannes. Out with it. Don't keep the old girl hidden away. Out with her."

It was three o'clock. We did not try to sleep at night anymore, because no one was safe in the dark, not even the little *Godafoss* from Iceland. During the day we rested—there was plenty of time then.

"What's he doing with his hand in his pocket all the time?"

"Take it out of your pocket, Hannes. Open your hand . . . go on, that's right."

"Empty! But he surely must be cheating all the same."

"You can pay me with some cognac, Pétur. It's nice to know about your money in my pocket."

The nights passed like this, one after another; we were

sailing without lights in the dark, trying to hide; Hannes was making money, I was breaking even, the rest were losing. The whole bunch. We would stare at the cards on the table between us and forget everything else: the table was a world where our own private war was being waged; no one but us was involved and fate was in our cards; the night passed as U-boats glided through the inky ocean, beneath our bunk beds, beneath our footing, but still far away.

I at once admired and envied Hannes. How he captured people's attention without the slightest effort. . . .

"Full house."

"Bastard!"

My little crime behind me and the convoy of ships wending its way like a serpent across the black surface of the ocean.

The metropolis.

We saw it from a distance before it grew light, watched it emerging from the night into the brown fog of daybreak. Everyone except the children had gone up on deck; we were standing there silently watching the stage gradually light up: the sky and the ocean and all that we imagined awaiting us beyond the fog. It was chilly, and we huddled closer to each other to keep ourselves warm, although without touching.

"How long are you going to stay, Hannes?" someone asked.

"A year. At least a year."

"What a difference leaving Iceland behind."

No reply.

"Of course there's a difference. You wouldn't be here if you didn't think there would be a difference."

Soon people would be waking up in the city. They would crawl to their feet and peep out through their curtains, rub the sleep out of their eyes, but take things slowly because of the dark. Have a wash and wake up the children. The son first. Boil some water to make coffee. Bachelors and fathers of two would shave and try to whistle familiar tunes at the same time (a wage rise the week before, a heavy meal last night), then start up and wash the shaving cream from their faces when they realize it is time to catch the train at the station on the corner. They would be late, much too late. . . . We were standing in a cluster, but not touching. It was blustery on deck and the lights ahead of us were cold.

"Where are you going to stay, Pétur?"

"I'm going to a hotel first. Then I'll see what happens."

"Let's try to meet up."

"Yes, we ought to keep in touch."

We exchanged goodbyes, our handshakes quick but firm. We were all traveling light except the Torfasons: they had a load of suitcases, large and small, old and new, and a trunk for good measure. More than once we had thought the woman would not last the journey.

"Nerves," said Hannes. "That's what it is."

He was the first to manage to hail a cab.

"Where should we meet up?"

"At that Icelandic restaurant Stjani was telling us about. Tomorrow night. Seven o'clock."

"Half past."

"Half past seven it is."

I took a cab to the boardinghouse Björn Franklin had told me about before I left. It was ten o'clock. I felt lost traveling through the city; a labyrinth, Hannes had called it. Skyscrapers, stores, hotels, cars and people: I could not see the people for the cars, nor the stores for the people, the sky for the skyscrapers. At the boardinghouse I managed to make myself understood, but my English was nothing to boast about.

Then I was on my way to the office on Fifteenth Street, on Björn's instructions. Everything would be ready for my arrival: a desk, a chair, a telephone and a secretary whom I would share with two others. I rummaged in my case and took out a business card from a blue box:

PÉTUR PÉTURSSON
Purchasing Representative

Franklin & Svensen
102 West 15th Street, 4th floor
New York 3, New York

"Purchasing Representative"—I twiddled the card between my fingers. Perhaps I really ought to anglicize my name: Peter. Plenty of time to worry about that. Peter Peterson.

The next day I was going to dine at the Icelandic restaurant Stjani had told us about. Hannes had given me the address. The first of many meals.

I have never felt comfortable in strange beds. It takes me a long time to fall asleep and I invariably wake up in the morning much earlier than I intend. It also takes me a long time to become accustomed to a new mattress or a new pillow: three, four weeks, sometimes longer. So it is not surprising that I dislike hotels and boardinghouses, which I avoid like the plague, and always have—except when I have had reason to visit them with women. But that has invariably been during the daytime, when I have had little intention of sleeping.

This was probably the reason I found myself an apartment to rent only a week after landing. It was a little place on the east side of the Park, but clean and conveniently located. I was very busy and I seem to remember that the thought of you never crossed my mind for the first couple of months. I met with Franklin & Svensen customers during the day, wrote letters, went to the bank, talked on the telephone and filled out orders. Thanks to the favorable terms we offered and our own growing confidence, our business flourished. In the evenings I met the lads at the Viking or some other restaurant or bar. I had most contact with Hannes and Stjani; I hardly remembered you at all anymore.

How did I manage to forget you? I have always lacked

a capacity for self-deception; no matter how I have tried, I am incapable of it. I am not easily surprised and never lose my composure, for I never encounter anything despicable that is unknown to me. You began to keep me awake at night and by day your image appeared when I least expected it. In the early hours I sometimes felt so much energy when I thought about my little crime that I could not remain still. Joyful energy. Then I would get out of bed, dripping with sweat, my face flushed, every nerve in my body tense, every muscle taut. I would pace the floor triumphantly until my passion subsided. The memory of my little crime was my monument; without it my humiliation would have been absolute. How could I live on hatred alone, you might ask. All these years. . . .

Hannes and I became close friends. He was the most intelligent of the lads who frequented the Viking, by far the most intelligent—the only one I could conceive of as a rival. Our contact increased steadily: we dined together, drank together, went to the movies together, consulted each other over business. Everything was rosy until one evening in early May, when I finally realized our friendship had become far too close.

If I recall correctly, it was a Friday evening. I had been working hard that week and was in high spirits at the weekend, for I had acquitted myself outstandingly in Franklin & Svensen negotiations with manufacturers. All goods were in short supply during those years and it was no easy matter to get hold of anything but the barest of necessities. I, however—I managed to secure more than the Icelandic importers had even asked for: sugar, flour, canned foods, biscuits, chocolate, electrical appliances—in other words, both necessities and luxuries. And since my superiors in Iceland had requested only a part of this bounty, I purchased the remainder myself and sold it to another exporter at a handsome profit. The same day! Sight unseen! To crown it all, the Viking was opening again after being closed for alterations for a week. There was plenty to celebrate.

I left work early and decided to walk home instead of taking a cab. I made a beeline up Fifth Avenue, tried on a suit in one store and a necktie in another, furtively bought a bottle of whiskey on Forty-fourth Street, enjoyed the fine spring weather and the Friday spirit of the people outside. When I got home, I put a record on the phonograph—Benny Goodman, if my memory is correct—took a long bath and drank whiskey on the rocks as I relaxed. It was nice, feeling the alcohol cleanse my mouth and throat on its way down, and the aftershave nipped my cheeks pleasantly. Hannes came by at half past six; we were flying high; we drank some more whiskey before setting off. Profound contentment that arrives unannounced and unexplained: how long has it been since I've known that feeling?

The Viking was crowded that evening: Stjani with two lads at a table near the entrance; a middle-aged man, a purchasing manager at H. B. Kjaran, sitting in the corner with three young women I had never seen before; students, fishermen, their friends and friends of friends at other tables.

"Hannes, you weasel," Stjani called out when we walked in. "So now you're going to eat with the money you won off me the other day?"

"Maybe you'd play better if you didn't talk so much," Hannes said.

Merriment, gestures of friendship, a hand placed on a shoulder—"Sit here with us"—the expectation of a good meal.

"I don't understand why you closed down for the week, Sigrid."

"Alterations. Necessary alterations. You can't have them done overnight."

"I can't see any difference. Hey, you guys, can you see any difference?"

"A complete overhaul," Sigrid said. "The whole works. As if you haven't noticed."

"She's right," said Stjani. "I believe they've swept the floor."

"I'll throw you out, you bums! You're not eating here!"

We had steak and potatoes. Some people were drinking wine, others water, still others whiskey. My body was tense after the long week, my mind reeling: "Cheers, you guys! Your health, madames et mademoiselles! More whiskey, Pete. You need some more whiskey to help wash down the steak."

I slowed down my drinking, feeling that I had already had one too many. Slowed down and guzzled one glass of water after the other. If you had been with me, we could have taken our leave and gone home. Perhaps we would not even have cared to mix with that crowd that evening, but would have gone out somewhere else by ourselves for a quiet dinner. I would have stroked the back of your hand while we waited for the waiter to bring the food, told you I loved you, promised that nothing would ever come between us. After the meal we would have walked the streets in the warm spring dusk, window-shopping; I would have asked you what you fancied. "This sweater, Pete, I'd love to have it." First thing next morning I go off and buy it for you. On the corner of Lexington and Seventy-seventh Street there is a florist open; I go in and buy a bouquet of roses for you. You kiss me on the cheek—"Look how lovely they are, Pete"—and the streetlight shines on your cheeks and soft hair and red lips. We walk slowly, holding hands. I am the happiest man in the world.

"Pete, are you drunk? You're completely ripped. Maybe a cup of coffee will help you sober up."

Myriad voices, singing and laughter all merge into a cacophony in my ears, reverberating inside my head. I buy you the biggest, prettiest roses in the shop. We walk home holding hands.

"Drink your coffee, Pete. It'll do you good."

"I can't."

"Just try."

"I feel sick."

"He's drunk, guys."

"I want to go home."

"Come on then. I'll help you find a cab," Hannes said.

It was warm and still outside. No breeze to rouse me from my stupor. Lights all around, yet I still could not figure out my surroundings.

"I need to vomit, Hannes."

"Wait, wait . . . I'll get a cab."

"I feel sick. I need to throw up."

He had no luck finding a taxi. I waited. Squatted down and waited.

"Let's walk. There aren't any cabs here. You can lean on me, Pete."

I do not know how long we walked. A haze around us,

wisps of fog, indeterminate sounds. At last I saw a car door open, felt myself being pushed inside and saw Hannes following.

"You're ripped," he repeated.

"I have to tell you something."

"Don't talk so much. You might make yourself sick."

"She deserved it."

"What are you talking about?"

"She deserved it after the way she treated me."

"Who?"

"In Copenhagen." (I clearly remember the difficulty I had pronouncing the name of the capital.)

"We're almost there. Don't start throwing up now."

"Promise you'll keep it a secret."

"What? Keep what a secret?"

"This is between you and me. You promise."

"Take it easy. Another half a minute. We're almost there."

"Hannes, you're my friend. She doesn't know it was me. I left the next day. In the morning. It was dark, Hannes. Pitch dark. . . ."

"You're out of it. We're here."

The cab door opened. I could hear Hannes asking the driver to wait, he was just going to help me in and would be right back. I went straight to the bathroom and threw up. I remained kneeling over the toilet bowl, waiting for the next eruption. I wiped the cold sweat from my face, hid my face in my hands and told him the whole story. Right from the start, when we were still in high school. Told him how you deceived and humiliated me. Told him how I felt when I was standing out in the street waiting to see your shadows merge into one, before the lights went out. Told him everything. In the minutest detail. Told him about my little crime. Even told him how I recoiled when I fired the gun. I cried uncontrollably and stood up to ask him to hand me a towel, but he was nowhere to be seen. I called his name, before gradually realizing I had not been telling my story to anyone but myself and the bathroom walls. I collapsed and fell asleep on the floor.

A long time passed before I met Hannes again. We had spoken on the phone occasionally, but I always avoided meeting him, citing the pressures of work and claiming that I was spending the little time I had left to myself with a woman. I trusted him even less than before. At that time I also began to have more dealings with business associates; among them was my friend John Lazarus. However, it was not until much later that my friendship with Hannes ended for good.

I still sleep in the same bed I did when I lived in that little place near the Park. Of course, I have had to change the mattress frequently, but I am quicker to adjust to a new mattress if the bed is the same. The mattress I sleep on now was bought more than five years ago. Really, I ought to start thinking about getting a new one. But somehow I have a feeling that I would not be able to enjoy such an investment for very long.

I am going to give myself a treat today, to mark nothing more than the fact that I slept well last night. I fell asleep watching *Casablanca* and did not wake up until dawn. I intend to celebrate the occasion in the evening—take a bath and have the girl massage my back afterward, dress in a light suit and white shoes, sport a blue handkerchief in my breast pocket, before looking at myself in the mirror and asking myself what wine I should offer myself: Graves or Saint-Émilion, Pauillac or Médoc, Margaux or Saint-Estèphe? Petrus or Lafite? Haut Brion '54 or Latour '61? Not answering immediately, I ponder awhile, fondle the Petrus '70 and wipe the dust from the Lafite '82, saying out loud that they are all good choices: '61 was a better year than '70, the spring cold with night frosts but the summer sunny and hot and dry in July and August; but the Petrus '70 is also a unique wine, soft as a young woman's skin, mature as the mother of generations and spared falling prey to the autumn rain. Eventually, I pamper myself by opening both bottles, since they obviously demand comparison. I light a candle and hold the bottle over the flame as I pour the wine into the carafe, taking care to leave the dregs behind, the Petrus first. Then I allow the wine to regain its composure after being moved, and to grow accustomed to the boisterous world outside the womb of the bottle.

I had slept well and was feeling energetic and replenished after the bath, and supple after the massage. Furthermore, there was a clear sky today and the proximity of the trees in the Park had a stimulating effect, and the tranquility that accompanies dusk was beginning to hint at its arrival. There will be a party tonight! I left the parlor for the study, thence to the dining room and kitchen, lit the candles, straightened up the books on the coffee table, opened the door to my wine cellar and added two candlesticks to the table where the wine was waiting, telling the girl to dress smartly. "There'll be a party tonight!" I said.

That night we were not going to dine in the kitchen or in front of the television, but in the dining room at the long mahogany table that my first wife bought in Brazil and my daughter covets. Since I was in a celebratory mood, I switched on the Christmas lights, which I never take down once the season is over, because contentment is not confined to a few days in December and January; no, it appears without the slightest warning, independent of seasons and motions of the clock, independent of birth and death, weather and wind, rules and regulations. I never store them away, because that would bring me down, remind me that all things must pass and there is no way to turn the clock back and alter what has already taken place. I unplug the lights when every festive occasion has passed, knowing that I can plug them back in whenever I like.

"Let us try some red wine before dinner," I said. "Would you prefer the Petrus 1970 or the Latour '61?"

Well aware that she had no knowledge of wine, I answered the question myself: "You would probably prefer the Petrus. It's a lighter wine. 'Sixty-one was a magnificent year."

Nimbly, I glided into the wine cellar and poured the Petrus carefully from the carafe into two glasses, the fluid rich and beautiful, a deep red tending to brown at its extremities. We raised our glasses by the oven. She was wearing a black skirt with a white apron while she cooked. I inhaled the scent of ripe fruit, plums, pears and cherries, chocolate, heather, spices and damp wood. She dipped her tongue into the wine as a gesture of companionship, even though she is not particularly partial to it.

"It's like traveling back in time and inhaling a whole summer," I said.

She smiled her half-smile, her eyes kindly, a memory of suffering somewhere deep behind them.

"What are you cooking, my dear?" I asked, making ready to look inside the oven to inspect it.

"A secret," she answered, gesturing to me to leave the oven alone.

"It must be something special. Lamb?"

"A secret."

"Lamb or veal?"

She shook her head to indicate that it was pointless for me to continue, smiling like a patient mother toward a boisterous son.

The candles were burning within, red ones in the parlor and white in the dining room and study; the Christmas lights were merry in the windows and over the doors between the rooms. I put Bach's Brandenburg Concertos numbers 1, 2, and 3 on the record player and could scarcely contain my inexplicable joy. No memories tonight, no images. You were forgotten and my little crime too, my ex-wives and children far away, stamina within my body and fine wine in my glass.

Tonight I'll do it at last, I told myself as she served roast duck with slices of orange and sweet berries. Tonight I have been given strength. Tomorrow no one will be able to tell her: "What are you hanging around that basket case for, a woman in her mid-twenties like you? You ought to get yourself a man your own age, a man who can keep you awake all night, make you thrash around and sweat, make your body tremble with pleasure. Why waste your time with that doddering old fool?" For I am young and strong today and she will wrap herself around me like the crown of a flower around a sunbeam; I shall feel her soft body merge with mine and relish listening to her breathing change. Afterward she will fall into a slumber and I will spread a dry sheet over her and wipe pearls of sweat from her forehead.

"Delicious," I said. "I don't think I've ever tasted such a fine duck. Where did you learn to cook duck so well?"

She answered with a shrug that she did not remember where she had learned to cook such a fine duck. "Would you like another slice?" she asked.

Another slice? You bet! And it's time for fresh glasses, even though our Petrus is still on the table, time to compare it with the Latour 1961: the color, the aroma, the bouquet on the tongue and in the throat, and its aftertaste.

"It's like comparing the sound of a violin and a cello first, and then their echo," I said, fetching the glasses.

No sooner had I left the table than the house intercom rang a long and insistent ring.

"Who could that be?" she asked.

"Just ignore it. He must have pressed the wrong button, that idiot of a doorman. You can never trust those Slavs."

"He's Irish," she said.

"Can't trust them either."

I arranged two balloon-shaped wineglasses on the table and went to the cellar to fetch the Latour, but was interrupted again before I had time to pour it.

"What a racket," I said. "He should have realized by now that he's ringing the wrong bell."

"Perhaps it is for you."

"We won't answer."

I kept my calm despite this interruption, stayed happy and animated as I reveled in the clarity of my mind. Just as I was about to lift the glass of Latour to my lips, the bell rang for a third time.

"He won't give up, will he?" I said. "I guess I should tell him to stop."

I took my glass with me to the hallway, inhaling the scent on the way and dipping my tongue into the wine, smacking my lips in delight and calling out to the girl that there was no way to tell which of the two wines was better, then whistled in accompaniment to Bach's second Brandenburg Concerto: *Allegro assai.*

"What a god-awful racket you're making, young man," I said on the intercom.

"It's not me, Mr. Peterson, it's your son. I told him you were out, but he ordered me to ring all the same."

"Dad, I have to talk to you!" I heard my son shout.

"Ask him what he wants," I told the lad.

I could hear rustling and indiscernible conversation for a fraction of a second, then my son snatched the phone.

"I really need to talk to you, Dad. It's Mom."

"You could have warned me instead of bursting in at this time of night."

"You never answer the phone, Dad. Can I come up?"

"We're eating. Can't it wait? Can't you go back home and call me from there. We'll probably be finished by then."

"She's ill, Dad. I don't want to stand here in the lobby telling you about it on the intercom. Let me come up."

"The only thing that's wrong with her is hypochondria. Go back to your wife and open a decent bottle of wine for yourselves. We're drinking Petrus '70 and Latour '61."

"I can't believe you're going to leave me standing down here in the lobby. She's in the hospital, desperately ill. . . ."

"You've always overdramatized everything, Helgi. Ever since you were a child. Always managed to make a mountain out of a molehill."

"Didn't you hear what I said, Dad? She's desperately ill. The doctors say she could go at any moment."

"Did she ask you to come here?"

"She didn't ask me anything. She's in a coma!"

Anguish in his voice, desperation and tension.

"Calm down, Helgi. You can't think straight when you're upset. She'll be strong as an ox tomorrow. Mark my words: strong as an ox."

"Let me come up."

"I'll slam this phone down if you don't stop shouting. Do you hear? What will the other people in this building think if they hear you? Act your age. You're behaving like a child. . . ."

Silence. I can hear his voice cracking.

"Just calm down. There's no need for you to come up. How's your wife? And the children—are they well?"

Wanting to avoid a scene in the lobby, I kept on talking to calm him down. I did not want him up here: that would only make things worse.

"Why are you asking me about my wife and children? You never ask about them. I doubt whether you can even remember their names."

"Of course I remember."

A nagger, that's what he's always been. Achieves nothing, soft and spoilt, but knows how to nag. And how I strove to make a man out of him. How I cared for him. A wimp.

"Mom's dying . . . and you're sitting drinking wine with that Chinese whore of yours."

"She's not Chinese. She's from Cambodia."

"Mom is dying, Dad."

"Pull yourself together, Helgi. Cut out the hysterics. Go and see her and phone me from the hospital. I want to find out how she's feeling. Is your sister with her?"

"Yes." His voice cracked.

"Go and see her and then phone me. Buy her some flowers from me on your way. I'll pay you back later. What does a nice bouquet cost?"

"You're unbelievable."

"What do you suppose one costs? But the price is irrelevant. Buy a nice bouquet and I'll mail you a check."

"I can't understand you. . . . She's dying! She's in a coma! Why the fuck are you going on about flowers when she's dying . . . ?"

"Helgi, let me tell you something you ought to pay attention to . . . Helgi . . . hello . . . Helgi?"

"He's gone, Mr. Peterson. He ran out."

I had to put my pen down early last night, I became so unsettled at recalling my conversation with my son. Helgi has always had a knack for unsettling me. Right from the start. I cannot remember his ever bringing joy to my home.

All the same, we did have pleasant times together in the past. I open the top drawer of my desk, reach for some old photographs in a brown envelope and take out the presents he brought me when he was a child. I contemplate the photographs: him sitting on my lap in my office with my pipe in his mouth. Of course, there is no tobacco in it, but he is wearing the profound expression men are supposed to have when they smoke a pipe, and John and I are smiling at him. There, we are putting up the Christmas decorations. There and there . . . I put the envelope back in the drawer, then distractedly fondle the presents he once gave me: the key from an alarm clock, a speckled blue pebble, a stick he had painted red and yellow.

The evening was ruined: the duck had gone cold, the candles burned down, the sauce stuck to the plate. The bottle of Petrus was half-empty, but the Latour barely sampled. All the joy had vanished. The Christmas lights were still on, yellow and red and blue; there were decorations of little houses, toboggans and white snow on the bells. The evening was completely ruined.

"I could heat up the duck again," she said.

But my appetite had disappeared and I could no longer taste the wine, the strength had leaked out of my body. Suddenly, I was drained.

"Should I make some coffee?"

Coffee would not pep me up; not coffee nor tea nor port nor cognac.

"That stupid fool, giving him access to the intercom. I've told him time and again not to let them near me."

She was silent. Cleared the table and put the plates in the dishwasher. Wiped the table and arranged the chairs around the dining table.

"The evening's ruined. Let's unplug the lights."

She obeyed, blew out the few candles that had not already burned and unplugged the Christmas lights.

"Do you want me to go rent a video? Is there a particular movie you'd like?"

Needing to be alone, I nodded, though I couldn't have cared less. I had realized early on that my son would not amount to much. But I did not expect him to be the weakling he is.

I took off my white shoes, undid my bow tie and unbuttoned my collar, placed my jacket over a chair and put on my slippers. I was waiting for the phone to ring. Would he be at the hospital by now? He must be there. But still he didn't phone. She has been playacting. A cold. Sore throat. Appendicitis at the very worst. She must have sent him.

I wandered into the study, the lights off, the party over. Bach was silent on the record player. I had planned to listen to Beethoven later in the evening while we were eating dessert: pears in port sauce. *Freude, schöner Götterfunken.* . . . Oh yes, isn't it just. I opened the refrigerator and looked inside. There were the pears; she had put them in a bowl and covered them with a plastic wrap to keep them fresh. Perhaps we will eat them tomorrow. Perhaps I shall feel better then. Tomorrow.

The telephone remained silent. I made sure the receiver had been put down properly; sometimes I take it off the hook when I want to be left in peace. It was secure, and I returned to the study and sat down by the window. Here I had planned to drink coffee and enjoy a glass of Rieussec Sauternes, inhale the aroma and recall the taste of honey, flowers, nuts and autumn. Here I had planned to make myself comfortable.

The clock struck nine, then half past nine. She returned with two movies in a bag, moving about quietly and taciturn as ever. She went into her bedroom to change, took off her dress and put on shorts and a white blouse. I had planned to follow her into her bedroom after the meal, dessert, and washing-up, I was going to turn the handle and open the door just as she was halfway out of her skirt; I was going to help her take it off, touch her lips and caress her hair, lie down with her on the unmade bed and show her that the blood was still flowing through my veins. But now I felt drained, the evening was ruined and it was pointless to think about pursuing her into her bedroom. I became bitter at the thought, suddenly clenched my fist, then released my fingers one by one as my hand rested on the edge of my chair.

At five to ten the telephone rang. It made me jump,

but I remained sitting; she could tell I had been expecting a call and hurried into the hallway to answer. She stopped when I called out to her to leave the telephone alone.

"He'll call back if he wants to do more than just nag."

She let the phone ring for a long time—five, six, seven, eight times—I trembled every time it rang—eleven, twelve—stop, I said to myself, no more, make that the last—thirteen times—silence. My body was like a taut string for the first few minutes afterward; having instinctively raised myself in the chair, I leaned back and mopped the sweat from my brow. *Wir betreten feuertrunken, himmlische dein Heiligtum. . . .* I had been planning to play the Ninth Symphony while I was eating the pears and drinking a glass of Rieussec; the choral movement would be on as I pursued her into the bedroom. *Alle Männchen werden Brüder . . .* and I would take her in my arms, her skin soft, her legs inching open . . . feel my muscles tightening, feel them, feel me, feel. . . .

A quarter past ten. It was nothing but nagging, I said out loud to myself. He would have phoned back if it had been anything more than nagging. He has never been able to tell the difference between essentials and irrelevances, a shower and a downpour, seriousness and joking. He has not turned out well, the poor kid.

By half past ten I was beginning to calm down. I asked the girl what movies she had rented. *The Big Sleep* and *The Maltese Falcon.* She knows I like Bogart. Which one should I watch first? I pondered for a moment but did not have the opportunity to make up my mind, for suddenly the telephone started ringing in the hallway. The girl went to the door.

"I'll answer," I said. "I shall answer."

I went over but did not pick up the receiver immediately, waiting instead a few moments, clearing my throat. My daughter was on the phone.

"I was expecting Helgi," I said.

"Helgi's here with me. Mom is dead. She passed away ten minutes ago."

"Why didn't you call before? Why didn't you let me know?"

"We phoned an hour ago, but you didn't answer."

"Where's Helgi?"

"He's here with me."

"Did she get the flowers from me? Did she know they were from me?"

"She never regained consciousness."

"But I asked him to. I begged him to. I told him to buy a nice bouquet and I would pay him back. I told him it didn't matter what they cost."

"She never regained consciousness."

"Where's Helgi?"

"He's here with me. We must go, Dad. They're putting her in a room where we can sit with her and say goodbye to her. They light candles. We're going to say goodbye to her."

"I was hoping she had gotten the flowers. I would have mailed Helgi a check."

"We must go now. Goodbye, Dad."

I took a long time to replace the receiver. There was silence in the apartment. Indescribable silence.

I did not think I should phone you, because you were doubtless still doing your morning chores. The couple you were staying with disapproved of your being disturbed when you were busy. They also disapproved of your being disturbed shortly after noon or early in the evening. You had told me that time and again. They appeared, in short, to abhor any kind of disturbance when you were doing your household duties. A petty-minded skinflint, you used to call the woman. Her husband, you would say, was grouchy and strict. You insisted I would have to wait until you phoned me. Otherwise you might have ended up in trouble.

It was only half past eight. A Saturday morning. I had not seen you since Tuesday and was starting to miss you. In point of fact, I had been missing you every minute since I said goodbye to you Tuesday evening and you had to run to catch the train home—if "home" is the right word. Half past eight and the autumn weather could not have been more beautiful: long, slender rays of sunshine in the streets and in the red and yellow leaves of the trees, on the windows of the bakery and the tiled roofs on the other side of the street; a light breeze ruffling the hair of passersby on the sidewalk, a few gnats on the windowpanes and the singing of birds close by. I lingered by the open window, watching the life on the street and the brightness from above. Someone was making coffee in the house and the aroma wafted toward me.

Half past eight. I was restless. We ought to have been out of the city by now, on the train north to where the forests spread out blue into the countryside, with sunshine playing on lakes and buzzing flies in a trail of dung on the roads; by now, you and I ought to have been standing under the heavy autumn tree, our blood agitated and a picnic in a bag: apples and sandwiches, cookies and beer. We ought to have been looking for a lake to sit beside or soft ground to lie on where the sun would have shone on our cheeks, your lips waiting for me to touch them. Half past eight and my landlady, a widow, had gone out to do her shopping; silence and dullness in the apartment, unrest magnified within my body.

I phoned. The woman answered. She was invariably polite and kind to me over the phone (that's nothing to go by, you said), asked me to wait while she fetched you from looking after the children in the garden.

"Let's go to the woods," I said.

"What's the time?"

"Nine o'clock. Today's your day off, isn't it?"

"Yes."

"I'll get a picnic ready," I said.

"I'll be around in forty-five minutes. You'll wait, won't you?"

"Of course I will."

I dashed downstairs and out into the street, to the bakery first and then the grocer's shop on the corner, bought some bread and ham and mayonnaise; went back home and made some sandwiches, wrapped them in waxed paper and put them in a paper bag along with four cookies, two apples and four bottles of beer. Opened the bag again when I realized I had forgotten the napkins, which I placed on top. It was like our first date: I was agitated, running rings around myself, mentally rehearsing over and over again what I would say to you and how I would say it, pondering sentences and words as if composing a verse in complex meter. Now and then I told myself to act natural, claimed that the words would issue effortlessly from my mouth when we were together, urged myself to show some self-confidence and manliness.

I felt everyone was watching you on the train: men and women, young and old, people our own age. We talked about the weather and our friends back in Iceland, Copenhagen, and the people you were staying with. You were in a happy mood that day. Happier than you had been for a long time.

"What's your college like, Pete?"

"It's okay."

"Only okay?"

"It will improve when I get to know more people and gain a better command of Danish."

"I'm speaking it well these days."

"You're with that family all day too. I'm just with my books."

"But your mother's Danish."

"That doesn't make any difference."

"You ought to try to meet more people. I can't understand why you haven't made any friends at college. You must like some of them. Surely you've met some girls you fancy. . . . "

Girls! As if you didn't know that I had come here to be

near you, to be able to spend evenings and weekends with you when you were not working. I was hoping to see you sometimes in the mornings and during the day. What good would friends do me? Why should I bother noticing other women? I had you.

We were approaching our destination. The city center behind us, old thatched houses on one side, golden cornfields on the other. Beyond the fields, deep dirt tracks meandered up and down the hills. You were talking. I was watching.

We walked into Frederiks Valley along the Princesses' Path and did not leave the track until we glimpsed a little lake inside the wood. It seemed remote; we ought to be able to be by ourselves there, I thought. We made our way through copses and thick trees, I walking ahead and you right behind me. The sun high in the sky: one o'clock. No one was around except the swans on the lake. Peace and quiet. In the distance, smoke was rising from a chimney on top of an old house. I had been there once and seen hunting bugles and old powder horns mounted on the walls, dressed leather pouches and shooting irons, and I knew we could go there if we needed anything. We lay down in a sheltered hollow by the lake. I was moderately tired after the journey and my body felt good. You spoke of how beautiful it was there.

"Look at the swans, Pete. . . . Look at the oak on the other side. Look how big it is. . . . Do you think we can go swimming in that lake? Do you think it's warm enough? It must be. . . ."

You babbled on and it was a delight to listen to you.

"Shouldn't we have something to eat first and rest a while before we go swimming?" I asked.

The sandwiches tasted good on an empty stomach and the beer was refreshing even though it was not cold anymore.

"Food tastes better outdoors, Pete. Don't you think so?"

My mouth full, I nodded.

"Who made the sandwiches?"

"I did."

"Really? Are you sure your landlady didn't?" A teasing note in her voice.

"Do you like them?"

"They're nice, Pete. How domesticated you've become. Maybe you ought to set up a sandwich bar."

I feared I was blushing, but wasn't. I smiled. I was in ecstasy.

After eating we lay on our backs and let the sun shine on our faces. I placed my palm on the back of your hand and entwined my fingers around yours. You opened your palm and stroked my thumb with your ring finger.

"What do you think we'll be like when we're old?" you said.

We were still lying on our backs; I could not see your face but was watching wisps of clouds scudding lazily across the blue sky.

"I don't know. Do you suppose we'll be any different from the way we are now?"

"Don't you think I'll grow ugly?"

I was starting to feel hot. My neck muscles tightened when I leaned my head back.

"I think you'll always be beautiful."

"You think I'm beautiful?"

It was difficult to talk with my head stretched back, but I still lacked the courage to look you straight in the face.

"Yes . . . you're the most beautiful person in the world."

You turned toward me and smiled. "What a sweet thing to say. How sweet of you, Pete."

You seemed to be stroking me more tenderly than before.

"Are you sure?"

"What?"

"Are you sure I won't grow ugly when I get older?"

I was on the verge of turning toward you and taking you in my arms but lost my nerve at the last moment. Reprimanding myself for cowardice, I vowed to look into your eyes and say I love you after mentally counting to ten.

You stood up before I reached five. You were wearing a swimsuit beneath your clothes; I saw that when you took off your shoes and socks, laid your blouse on a white rock and your dress too.

"Come on, Pete!" you called as you ran into the water.

I hurried to join you. We frolicked in the water, laughing, splashing and chasing each other. The lake was shallow close to its banks, but suddenly deepened farther out. I dived and surprised you by grabbing your toes and presenting you with a string of weed that I clenched between my teeth. The water was not warm, but our bodies adjusted to it quickly and the rays of sunshine crept through the branches of the trees around us.

Before I knew it, you were in my arms. We looked into each other's eyes momentarily; it was as if we were astonished at what was taking place. We kissed. I put my arms around you and pressed you tightly against me, hoping I would never need to let you go. Every nerve in my body was taut when you swam away from me, laughing. That soft skin . . . I chased you.

I gathered a bunch of flowers and gave them to you before we left. Our hair was wet, our bodies comfortably tired, and the sun going down when we set off for home. Walking by your side, I extended my hand to you. Our fingers touched.

The earth was preparing for its nightly sleep. Farmers returning home from fields. You smiled at me in the light that glittered through the leaves of the trees. That moment, no one in the world felt as good as I did.

Since you had time off that evening, we decided you would come home with me to take a bath. I stayed in the sitting room with my landlady while you bathed and dressed. Your blouse had become rumpled and damp in the course of the day, so you packed it in your bag and put on one of my shirts that I had laid out for you. It was a blue-striped cotton shirt that suited you well once you rolled up the sleeves. You were flushed after your bath and somewhat tanned; I stood as close to you as possible, to inhale your scent. Then you waited with the old lady while I took my bath; she was always pleased when someone took the trouble to chat with her.

Both hungry, we decided to go out to eat at one of the restaurants nearby. You led the way. We were holding hands. The streets were lit and so were windows everywhere, but the autumn twilight mellowed the lights as if they were veiled.

"What do you fancy, Pete?"

"I don't care. It's up to you."

"You're more familiar with this part of town than I am. You choose."

"There's plenty to choose from. Why don't you decide?"

You started acting as if I had laid a heavy burden on

your shoulders as you frowningly scrutinized every establishment we passed: one was too expensive, the next too squalid, the third too stuffy. I delighted in watching you: your expressions, your walk, your hair as it started to dry after your bath.

"What do you think of this place, Pete? Isn't it nice? Hm, maybe a bit too nice. All the men wearing suits and ties and the women in dresses. Nice for some, anyway."

You were a woman of decorum, for sure. You knew I was paying, but you still chose a place in accordance with your own limited means. Eventually, we sat down at a small but smart restaurant on a side street a little way from the Church of the Holy Ghost. I remember the whitewashed walls and the waiters in blue shirts with white aprons and bright-colored bow ties. It was neither quiet nor noisy, neither stuffy nor pretentious. The guests were of all ages, but most of them older than us. I ate meatballs with potatoes and peas, you had the chicken. The food was reasonably priced and the beer was cheap. We talked about everything under the sun: the weeds in the lake, the food, the approaching autumn. As usual, you talked more than I did, which I liked, for I enjoyed hearing the sounds of your voice. When we fell silent, it was by no means uncomfortable, but more a confirmation of our relationship; friendship and. . . . We sat there until almost eleven, when I paid the check and we strolled out into the encroaching darkness. I tossed a coin into the hat of a fiddler on the sidewalk when we paused to listen to him play. Everything was gentle and calm: the moon in the sky, the food in my stomach, the glow left by the sun on my body and the warmth of the autumn dusk. And you by my side as if you had always been there and would never leave.

I walked you to the station just after eleven o'clock. Your hair was dry by then. I ran my fingers through it and gave you a long kiss.

"This is the way I want it to be. . . . Forever. . . . I want you to be with me until I die."

"Oh, Pete. Don't be so serious. We shouldn't get too serious now. It's been such a wonderful day."

"I've never felt so good. I don't think I can ever be without you."

"Oh, Pete. . . ."

The train left at twenty past eleven. You waved to me from the window until you disappeared from sight. Instead of going straight home, I stood on the platform awhile staring into the darkness that had enveloped the train. "We shouldn't get too serious," you had said. "We." That implied a common interest, that we were contemplating the same thing, because you said "we," not "you."

Eventually, I wandered off home, imagining your face as the train pulled out.

I do not care to waste ink describing what a child I was in those years. What a simpleton. There is no need. It irritates me not to have grown up earlier.

A long time has passed since this happened. I have not seen you for half a century. I ought to have remembered your mother when you asked me if I thought you would be ugly when you were old. That poor woman:grotesquely fat, her eyes lost in her face, mouth gaping. I should have listened when people said how much you resembled her when she was young. I often used to see her from a distance when we were growing up. Reykjavik was no big city in those days. She was always chattering away. Could not shut up. Chattering away. Even in the theater during performances. Vain. You could see it a mile off.

Surely you don't resemble her in your old age. That would be ironic! I have always imagined you just as you were the last time I saw you. In my memory you have remained the same. Not aged a year, not a day older. Eternally young. How great is the power of self-delusion.

I do not even know if you are still alive. If you are, I do not know where you might be. In my mind's eye you are still a girl of twenty with dark hair, short and straight, your body slim and curvaceous, your eyes sparkling, your skin soft.

You left me many clues that evening. Yet I was still convinced that we were about to start a long, intimate life together. I could not imagine the set behind the curtain. But clearly there was much going on there.

Breasts droop, waists sag, dresses get larger. Each and every day brings us closer to death. This we can see in the gray hair we have not noticed before, feel in a fresh bout of rheumatism, notice in the wrinkles that we have formed beneath the right eye. Longer shadows. Less sleep.

Here I await dawn, an old man. Give me a few weeks more, an iota of strength, the peace of mind to talk to myself in solitude.

The funeral will be held today. Both children tried to get me to go and pay my last respects, but I told them I was not in good enough health. I did not make this up: I have been unwell the past few days. Ever since she died.

It had never entered my mind that I would outlive her. I still have trouble believing she is dead. The day before yesterday I entertained a suspicion that her apparent death was part of a byzantine plot by her and the children. The three of them have always been ready to close ranks against me. I could imagine her roaring with laughter when Helgi told her I had been taken in by the ploy. The thought so enraged me that I took to bed. The girl brought fruit juice for me to drink and I soon calmed down. I grew pensive as I lay there: How could I possibly have entertained such an idea? That my own children would lie to me about their mother being dead? Why was I sometimes such a monster?

Our marriage was nothing for her to boast about. She lived for almost thirty years with a man who did not love her. The marriage was devoid of passion from the outset, mundane, insipid. Yet I never treated her badly in the conventional sense, was never violent toward her, neither physically nor psychologically. For instance, I never told her I did not love her. All the same, I suspect she soon began to sense it. My countless one-night stands with other women—I tried to conceal them from her, knowing they would upset her. She was not a complex personality: her conversation was banal, her intellect limited. She was a typical middle-class American woman, a doctor's daughter, her view of life in accordance with conventional standards and a professed fear of God, both of which were infantile and slightly pretentious. She was happy if her children were healthy, the weather fine, and there were no foreseeable disruptions in her daily life. When she was younger, she was coy in bed and uninventive. We stopped sleeping in the same bed when Helgi reached his teens. I cannot remember exactly how it came about, but I am certain that it happened without any scenes or flared tempers. She was perhaps only following an accepted code of behavior that she had learned since childhood. I could not have cared less. She always had dinner served at seven o'clock, wanted us to take our vacations in July, arranged her days and her life as if managing an assembly line. She could not put up with any sort of unreliability or chance, disorder or coincidence, wanted everything to conform to a fixed pattern. She governed the home. I lived as I chose. She never had to worry about money; I had no reason to fear that she would squander it.

I have nothing to complain about as such. I know a man who has gone blind. He misses nothing as much as being able to read the newspapers. He buys them every morning simply so that he can smell the paper and ink. He sits with the papers in his lap while drinking his morning coffee, fumbles with one hand for the sugar bowl and eats a sugar lump while opening the paper and turning the pages with the other. His maid is Mexican and does not speak English. His wife refuses to read to him. She says she is avenging his unfaithfulness to her, for a total of five months, forty years ago. When she wakes up one morning to find him dead by her side, she will ask herself whether such vengeance was worthwhile. And each and every morning afterward she will ask the same question, unable to do anything to change what has come to pass.

Our divorce was in keeping with the rest of our relationship: untumultuous. When the children left home, it became increasingly clear that our marriage was merely cosmetic. I once mentioned briefly that perhaps it would be best to call it a day, and never referred to the subject again, knowing that I had no need to do so. She was too proud to wait for my initiative. A week later she called a lawyer. She saw no reason to go on with the charade, she said, now that the children were grown up. If that's what you want, I said, I'm not going to stop you.

No one knew better than I her torment within. Her life had been destroyed, everything she believed in was shattered: family, routine, marriage. We arrived at a quick settlement, free of conflict. She received her due; I was in no way dishonorable, even though I made sure I did not have to pay any more than I was obliged to, a reasonable sum.

The funeral will be held at two o'clock. I am too weary to go pay my last respects. The windows are flung wide open in my bedroom and the study as well, but the air indoors is still heavy. I never expected to outlive her. I had always imagined her dressed in black beside my coffin, with Helgi to her left and Gudrún to her right. That was the way I imagined it: their feigning mourning at my funeral followed by long meetings with my lawyer. The inheritance: How much has the old bastard left behind? How big is our share? She provided for the children, safeguarded their interests. For herself she needed little but would have walked over red-hot coals for them.

They are coming to visit me at noon. I cannot forbid them doing that, since I shall not be attending the funeral. But I do not look forward to seeing them. No, I dread their arrival.

It rained last night and this morning. I hope the humidity will disappear and it will brighten up this afternoon. Her send-off deserves a bit of sunshine.

If I lean back and turn my head to my left, I can see the sky through a gap in the curtains between the two skyscrapers on the next block. The sky seems to be clearing up; at least I caught a glimpse of blue between the buildings a moment ago. But I cannot take a long look out of the window, because I tend to get a stiff neck if I am not careful.

For dust thou art . . . and unto dust shalt thou return. . . . Perhaps the sun will come out for the funeral. I sent flowers. For once, I did it myself, instead of relying on Helgi. I hope I manage to avoid seeing him and his sister again during the short time I have left.

I am still agitated after their visit. Yet two hours have passed since they left. I had to lie down, the girl was going to call a doctor, but I forbade her from doing so. Helgi was in a dark suit, with a blue-striped tie. He was pale and weary, with circles beneath his eyes. He seemed to be walking unsteadily. Gudrún was wearing a black dress, golden earrings and a necklace, as if she were on her way to a dance. She acted detached and seemed to be daydreaming while she was sitting in the parlor. I advised the girl to stay in her own bedroom for the duration of the visit.

"I wish I could go with you to pay her my last respects," I said. "I never expected her to go before me."

Helgi was sitting beside his sister like a little boy, head bowed and in silence, alternately twisting his fingers together and unfolding them.

"Never expected it would turn out like this."

I searched for the right words and emphases like an actor on a stage. I knew what I was supposed to say and how I was supposed to say it. My role had been determined long before. All I needed to do was find the right words.

"Even though we went our separate ways, I always respected your mother. Whatever I might have said in moments of thoughtlessness or anger, I always liked her. . . ."

It was like listening to someone else talking, like sitting by the radio listening to a play. I was hoarse after a troubled night, and my voice was low. Whether it was part of my playacting I cannot tell, but suddenly I felt tears running down my cheeks, first from my right eye, then from my left. Caught unawares, I did not know how to stop weeping. In the end, the tears began to pour down my cheeks like water along the course of a long-since-dried-up river.

The children sat dumbfounded with astonishment; through my tears I could see them exchanging panic-stricken glances. I doubt whether they had ever entertained the notion that I could break down in front of them and reveal my weaknesses and failings. They saw my old face wrinkle up and my body tremble like a blade of grass in the wind. Their world had been turned upside down. Their father was no longer a villain and a perpetrator of evil, but a sick old man, a broken wretch who had destroyed his happiness through violence and greed. How could they help but feel sympathy for him? Gudrún was tougher and more obstinate than Helgi, who could not bear to watch my misery and pain.

"Dad," he said. "Oh, Dad. . . ."

In desperation, he clutched my shoulder and leaned his head against my brow. I could feel a wet cheek touching me.

"Why didn't you come, Dad?"

I had stopped crying, and I eased him carefully away from me. His softness has always irritated me. Instinctively, I bristled at his face bloated with tears.

"Where?"

"To see Mom in the hospital. Why didn't you come when I asked you to?"

I could feel that I was losing control of myself. Did they come here to make accusations and settle what they saw as old scores? I stood up, went over to the window and ordered myself to keep calm. Those weaklings. Never achieved anything and will leave nothing behind them. It would have changed nothing had they never existed.

"You didn't even let me in when I came here to see you. . . ."

I felt I was going to explode. My hands were shaking with rage, my veins swelled and I could feel the heat welling up in my face.

"Jerk!" I shouted. "You make me ashamed to call you mine! Look at yourself . . . a man in your forties . . . take a look in the mirror . . . you've always been a wimp! You've never bothered to make the effort to grow up into a man! Your wife orders you about! Your sister orders you about!

You come here on the day of your mother's funeral and act like a child. Like a spoiled kid. . . ."

I was groping for words. The more repulsive they were, the faster I incorporated them into my disjointed tirade.

"But Dad. . . . " he stammered. "How can you say that, Dad?"

"Never made any effort! Neither of you! Always known the old man has bags of money. You've never done anything but wait. Wait for me to drop dead. I used to imagine you with your mother beside my coffin. 'Now he's dead! Roll out the barrel!' But she got out first. Didn't expect that, did you? I can tell how confused you look, Helgi. Who's going to hold the little boy's hand now?"

"He's crazy," Helgi said to his sister, as if I were not present. "He's gone crazy."

"You'll get nothing from me. Not a cent! You couldn't even get up off your butt to buy your mother some flowers, like I asked you over and over. It was asking too much to expect you to drop in at the florist's on your way to the hospital."

I went on and on. I could not restrain myself—did not try to restrain myself, but went on and on, I don't know how long.

Helgi pleaded with his sister: "Ask him to stop . . . make him stop. . . . I can't listen to it anymore. . . . Mom's dead. . . ."

Gudrún had been listening silently, except for the occasional whispered "Repulsive." At last she stood up and took her brother by the arm. I could feel my heart thumping in my chest. I was panting, as if I had been fleeing a pursuer.

"Get out! Piss off!"

"I hope you realize that you're sick, Dad," she said as they walked to the door. "I hope you realize you're not in control of your faculties. We're off. We won't be disturbing you in the future."

Helgi stood in the doorway. His eyes were like a wounded animal's.

It has been raining during the funeral.

Why did their visit have to turn out this way? I had planned to be frank with them, and understanding, told myself before they arrived that it was time to bury the hatchet. Instead, we clashed more fiercely than ever before. I regret having said what I said, although I can argue that I was justified. But the truth is often best left untold—especially on the day of my ex-wife's funeral.

I was going to say to them: "Let's forget all the bad feeling from the past few years, act as if nothing has ever happened that might come between us. Let's forgive each other. Forgive . . . unconditionally. Your mother has passed away; it's a great loss for all of us. I know that she was not fortunate in her choice of me as a husband, but there is nothing to be done about that now. All the same, I want you to know that I always liked her. We had a lot of happy moments together when we were young. We even had good times together later. Your mother was a good influence on me: she brought order to my life, made a beautiful home for us, gave me the support that every man needs in order to get ahead in his work. Behind every successful man is a woman. Beside him, not behind him, beside him, I mean. That's the way it is, my children, whichever way you look at it.

"Now that she has passed away, there's nothing left but for us to stick together. I want to help you do something positive. I know I shall never be a substitute for your mother, but I want to do what I can to be of help to you. Maybe you need some money to put your plans into practice? Maybe you're a bit short of cash? Come to me. I'm not suggesting that I'm willing to throw money out the window, you understand, but I would like to give you a helping hand if you need one. Helgi, go and choose yourself a few good bottles of red wine from the rack in the cellar. You can drink them with your dinner. I'll never finish them myself. I'm too old now. Go and get a bottle of, say, Cos d'Estournel 1984. It is supposed to be very pleasant, even if the vintage was nothing special. Wines from a lean year often make better table wines. Good harvests are always heavy and take a long time to mature. Big wines are too independent to behave properly with a meal. Just like pianists: when they think they're virtuosos, they play solo instead of accompanying the singer. But that's another story, of course.

"Tell me, Gudrún, won't your son William soon be thinking about college? Starts next year, does he? I thought so. Can you afford to send him to a decent place? There's no sense in sending him anywhere but a top-rate college. Just let me know how I can help you out. I regard it as an investment—an investment in the future of the family. We have to stick together. . . ."

They would have thrown their arms around me in gratitude; I would have seen the twinkle in their eyes, like a long-dormant spark awakened by an unexpected gust of wind. They would have chastised themselves for their negligence and vanity, their disrespect toward me and their blind lust for my money. I would have forgiven them.

"That's all in the past," I would have said. "Let's think about the future."

They would have kissed me on the cheek before leaving.

"Take care of yourself, Dad."

"Remember to pay her my last respects as well. I wish I could go with you."

"You're too frail, Dad. Take things easy so you'll get better quickly."

"Pay her my last respects, remember."

But that was not the way it turned out; it is uncertain whether that would have been possible. I threw them out. They hinted they might never visit me again.

My days are running out. It has been pouring incessantly for the past couple of hours. Every now and then there is a clap of thunder: streaks of lightning momentarily illuminate the grayness, and the windowpanes rattle. I begin to feel afraid, wondering whether it will ever clear up again.

D own the west side of Copenhagen's Købmagergade, not far from the Round Tower, there is a side street that few people ever notice. Not only is it short and narrow, but it has no stores or restaurants to attract crowds. Most people appear to think the street is nothing more than an alley or driveway, a venue for delivery trucks by day and cats and tramps by night. But the fact is that on this unassuming street there is one of the most interesting bookstores in all of Copenhagen, for those who have the patience to wend their way by the back doors of restaurants and two barber shops before reaching it. On the ground floor there are recently published books on the shelves and tables; coffee and cakes are on sale in one corner too. The upper floor, on the other hand, is antiquarian. It is a rare pleasure to pore over its dusty tomes, as one holds a coffee cup in one hand while the sweet aftertaste of Danish pastry lingers in the mouth. The store is rarely crowded, but never deserted either: just a reasonable number of people, so that you never feel cramped, but never lonely either.

The first time we went to the bookstore, there were uncommonly few customers there (three besides ourselves, if I recall correctly), for it was midmorning and most people were going about their daily business. I was becoming interested in books at this time, especially books about history and philosophy. You, by contrast, read all kinds of fiction, sometimes pulp and sometimes what are called literary works.

When I felt depressed by accountancy, by all the debits and credits, and was on the verge of leaving my humdrum business school for more palatable pursuits, it sometimes took no more than a visit to the B. Andersen & Sons bookstore to cheer me up. I relished the thought of my fellow students in their pathetic classes on double-entry bookkeeping while I was thumbing through first editions, perhaps on the philosophy of Kant, perhaps on thirteenth-century history, that dark age of sorcery and retribution.

In the evenings there were often gatherings on the ground floor. Scholars and writers would read from their works, the audience would sit on hard chairs and imbibe a wealth of knowledge and deep wisdom; then there would be a break. All present would stand up and stretch their legs, buy coffee and cake, compare notes and shake the speaker's hand. Since then I have often marveled at how unpretentious these gatherings were: no histrionics, the timbre of the speakers' voices generally pleasant. The audience had come to listen. Not to see and be seen, but to listen.

We were going to meet there at eight o'clock. Admittedly, I had had to press you somewhat, but that was all part of it, of course, and in fact I enjoyed it to some extent. You said you were not sure whether you could take time off that evening, since the couple was thinking of going to a concert. Besides, you were feeling under the weather after sleeping badly the previous night, fighting off a headache until the early hours. But I would not yield, promised that

an interesting reading would make you feel much better—
Kelvin Lindeman, I said, weren't you reading a book by
him the other day? Eventually, we agreed to meet at B. Andersen & Sons just before eight, which you preferred to my
meeting you at the train station, because we might have
missed each other in the crowd. I had been looking forward to seeing you all day, found it difficult to concentrate
on what I had to learn (if "learn" is the right word for such
elementary sums), wondered whether you would wear
your hair loose or in a ponytail (I thought it looked nicer
loose), tried to guess how you would be dressed.

I turned up at quarter to eight. The store was open and
I went in and bought you the author's latest book, beautifully bound, and had it wrapped in blue paper. It was cold
outside, well into November, calm but cold with snow
forecast that weekend. While I was waiting, I read a letter
that I had received from Mother that day: No news worth
telling, everyone keeping as well as might be expected. Father was suffering from occasional bouts of rheumatism but
that was nothing new. My sister had become engaged to an
offspring of the Reykjavik bourgeoisie, someone I had
seen at dances, of average intelligence and harmless
enough. The bourgeoisie—perhaps I had been reading too
much political thought the past few weeks. Father was
going to invest in a new car for Christmas. P.S. from Father: "Look after yourself. Get plenty to eat. Let me know
if you need anything. Everything is fine at this end. What
do you think of your sister's suitor?" I stuck the letter in my
pocket.

You were wearing your hair loose as I had hoped, were
dressed in a red skirt, a thick coat, a white sweater showing
underneath. You had put your hat in your coat pocket be-

fore entering the store. We greeted each other with a smile; I did not know whether it was *de rigueur* for me to greet you with a kiss, other people being present. You were not weary or sleepy in the slightest, but rosy-cheeked and a little out of breath after your walk, and you brought freshness and cheer into the building.

The reading was uneventful; I hardly listened, so focused was I on you by my side; you were wearing a new perfume, your scent was enticing but not overbearing. Nothing escaped your attention, neither the words of the author nor the movements of the people around us: "Look at that couple in the front row. You can tell it's the first time they've ever gone out together. Look how nervously they're holding hands. . . . He's shy. He doesn't know whether to hold on or let go. . . ." You were right: the man was hesitant. I whispered to you that you were a keen observer of human nature, without imagining for an instant that you must have scrutinized me with the same eyes as you did everyone else. "He's terribly shy," you would doubtless say to yourself, "childish, dithering. . . . When's he going to get down to business? When will he offer me more than a goodnight kiss? When will he brace himself, take me back to his place on a quiet afternoon, draw the curtains, throw me down on the bed and run his hands all over me? When?"

"You're right," I said in my naïveté. "He's unsure about how to behave."

I, trapped in your web of deception, passing judgment on a version of myself just a few yards away! You must have laughed to yourself, no question about that. Laughed yourself sick.

Just before nine o'clock there was a break. We went

outside, sipping our coffees, to breathe some fresh air. It was cloudy; snow was forecast. I was lightly dressed, having left my coat inside, but I still enjoyed the cold so close to the doors that led back to the warmth. You told me you hoped the reading would finish before ten, because you had to be home early. I promised there would not be a single light left on in the store by ten o'clock.

"He'll be finished well before ten," I said. "Don't you worry."

I noticed toward the end of the second half of the program that you were fidgeting in your seat. Your eyes began to roam around the room, your concentration lapsed. You kept looking at your watch. I put my arm around you and patted you on the shoulder: "There's plenty of time. Take it easy."

When the reading finished, without waiting for the applause to die down you rose and put on your coat.

"That was fun," you said with a brisk smile.

When we reached the door, I noticed you had forgotten the book I had given you. It was still on the chair where you had been sitting, and I rushed back to fetch it.

"You forgot the book," I said.

"How silly I can be sometimes."

"You haven't read it already, have you?"

"No, I've been meaning to buy it for a long time. I just forgot it in my rush. I promised them I would be back early. How silly I can be sometimes."

I said that it could have happened to anyone.

"Thanks," you said, kissing me on the cheek.

I walked to the station and you said a hurried goodbye outside.

"I must hurry," you said, "the train's leaving."

You kissed me twice, as if you considered the first too short and abrupt. The second was a bonus.

I walked back home, the bonus on my cheek, my hands in my pockets; I quickened my pace to stay warm. I had half-expected you to stay longer, thought I would have a chance to take you to a coffeehouse or pub after the reading. I was not in the mood to go straight home.

Earlier that day the other students had invited me to join them at the Little Apothecary pub after dinner, which I naturally turned down, but now I decided to see if any of them might still be there drinking. I wouldn't be surprised if it starts snowing, I said to myself; it's not as chilly as the past few days, but gloomy with a hint of precipitation in the air. Warmed by my walk, I strolled on a whim past a fishing-tackle shop I had a fondness for. Reels from Sweden, Hardy and Milward rods: they could come in handy on a boat out on a lake. And those flies—get a load of those flies and spoons arranged in organized chaos on the windowsill on the inside of the window.

Just before I reached the pub, I felt the first snowflakes fall on my forehead, big flakes that glided to earth in the calm weather. I have always experienced bliss at the first snowflakes of winter, a childlike glee I cannot explain but can control. On that occasion I did no more than stick out my tongue, the snowflakes melting the moment they landed on it. There were not many people about, and I managed to walk the last few paces to the pub with my tongue sticking out and no one noticing me.

The windows of the pub were steamed up; it was clearly crowded inside. Guffaws came through the door, shouts and laughter, praise and abuse. I took off my coat as soon as I got inside, and folded it over my arm. There were people standing at the bar and wherever else there was room; people were sitting at every single table, in fact on top of one or two of them. A haze of smoke in the air and a heavy stench of beer. I did not notice my fellow students in the throng. I suppose I could see only a quarter of the tables or so from where I was standing, so I squeezed my way toward the bar in the hope of a better view. Nudges, sweat, steam and haze: I had still not become accustomed to Copenhagen's much-vaunted watering holes. Would I ever grow accustomed to them? At long last I reached the bar.

Just as I was attempting to order a beer from the bartender, I noticed you sitting at a table by the window. At first I tried to persuade myself that I was seeing things, but soon had to yield my ground: that was you, in your white sweater and red skirt. You whom I had said goodnight to half an hour before. You who were supposed to be on a train heading for the suburbs where you lived. You who said you were in a hurry because you had promised to get home early. You!

There were four of you at the table, you and another girl I did not know and two young men. I did not recognize them either. I could not make out a word—it was far too noisy—but there was no question that you were in good spirits. You were laughing with your girlfriend, laughing out loud, and every so often you cast an admiring glance toward one of the two men. I thought they were Icelanders, although of course I could not be certain.

I do not know how long I stood at the bar looking in your direction—ten seconds, twenty seconds, half a minute? I felt sick. I had a lump in my throat. Sweat, stench and foul air; I could have thrown up on the spot.

When you leaned toward him and whispered in his ear, I could see how he put his hand around your shoulder. He had done that before. He had touched you before. I could see that. Acting as if he owned you!

I shoved my way toward the door, pushing aside everyone in my path, lashing out, had to get out. I did not start walking when I emerged on Kannikstrade, did not put on my coat, but ran into the darkness and falling snow, ran aimlessly, no direction in mind.

What was the weather like in the last week of November and the first week of December in 1939? I must confess I cannot remember. I have no clue. Yet I had little else to occupy me during those weeks than sitting at home, staring into the air and trying to find some explanation for your behavior. I attended school rarely at that time, read little, felt too bad to absorb the principles of accounting, debit and credit, arithmetic for ogres. Noticing I was not eating, my landlady decided I was probably ill, in all likelihood suffering from some bug that was going around. At first I was not only hurt but angry, furious, and vowed never to speak to you again. I had planned to ignore you when the chance arose, to pretend I did not know you if I ran into you, refuse to help you out even if you were in need and implored me in your distress. I told myself time and again that I did not give a damn about you, you meant nothing to me, there were countless beautiful and elegant women in the world who would not object to getting to know me—many of them easily within my reach. Sometimes I would fake casual laughter and say out loud: "Damned bitch, she sure is crafty. Really took me for a ride!"

But no matter how much I laughed to myself, how often I tried to drum into my head that this short and insignificant chapter in my life was over and that the time had come to start thinking about more constructive things, it never worked. I thought of you during my sleepless nights, woke up with an aching stomach, felt terrible all day, terrible beyond words. On the fifth day I found myself trying to find out why you visited the pub, find a harmless explanation that would make me feel better and convince me there was nothing to stop me from picking up the telephone and calling you. Perhaps you had unexpectedly bumped into your girlfriend after saying goodbye to me; perhaps your girlfriend had pressed you to go with her and you had been unable to refuse; perhaps you had missed the train and had gone to ask your girlfriend to put you up for the night; perhaps, perhaps. . . . That's what must have happened, I told myself, there's no more plausible explanation than that. On the eighth day I was on the verge of picking up the phone until I realized you had not bothered to call me for more than a week. Not wondered about me; it hadn't crossed your mind to see how I was doing. For the past week you behaved as if I did not exist.

In fact, you had never contacted me on your own initiative anyway; instead, you waited for me to pester and pamper you. So this was nothing new. But still . . . still I did not think you showed very much affection for me when you did not even phone to thank me for the evening at B. Andersen & Sons bookstore and for the book I had given you. No, I did not think so. But perhaps you had been unusually busy those days; who knows if the people you were staying with disapproved of your not coming home after the reading, as you had agreed you would, and decided to punish you for it?

I argued the ins and outs of the situation to myself,

playing the prosecution and the defense at the same time, the jury and the judge. I swung from one extreme to the other, flying into a rage at you and pitying you by turns, asserting in one breath that you were a worthless shrew and in the next that you had committed no other crime than to miss the train on a cold night, alone in a big city on a winter night with a snowstorm about to begin. On the fourteenth day I delivered my pronouncement: you were not guilty of all charges but had simply missed the train. The sentence was not only mild but downright convenient: I phoned you immediately.

You spoke as if nothing had happened, although admittedly you asked me why I had not been in touch for two weeks, but in other respects you made no mention of anything but the same run-of-the-mill events as usual. But you did say you met some other Icelanders that you would like me to get to know. Said they were a lively crowd whose company I would doubtless enjoy. Pleading a heavy workload from my studies and a touch of the flu, I told you how I had intended to phone you but never managed to do so because I had been so busy. We agreed to get together on Friday evening: I would meet you at the train station at eight o'clock.

The trial over and all parties satisfied, the misunderstanding rectified. Once again I could begin looking forward to spending an evening with you. I was in seventh heaven.

Since then I have often wondered why you kept on playing your game as long as you did. Did he know about me? Did you tell him about me? For a long time I doubted that you had, but I was still uncertain. Would that not have lessened the thrill? You said goodbye to me and went to him, said goodbye to him and came to me. And as time passed, we increasingly happened to meet in crowds. That was the way you must have wanted it too: more thrills, close calls.

To dispel all misunderstanding, I must of course make it plain that you did not treat the two of us entirely in the same manner. Far from it. The pain, the first time I followed you back to his place and watched the lights go out in his window.

On the south end of Central Park, near the corner of Fifty-eighth Street and Sixth Avenue, there is a little restaurant which I think is called Jean Lafitte. In the lobby are a bar and a few tables where you can sit and drink a cold gin and tonic on hot days. There are bowls of nuts on the tables too. Farther in, in a dark room, meals are served.

During the summer they set tables up on the sidewalk, for the front window is really a sliding door. At the bar itself there are high stools with red seats for people who can't find an empty table or prefer to be left in peace with their drinks and magazines. They can turn their backs on the other guests and shut them out. The furnishings are beginning to look worn, the wood on the tables is cracked and the paint is fading on the walls, but everything is clean and tidy all the same, with a sense of time-honored solidity in the air. The music is always quiet and pleasant to the ear: French songs and other light music from Europe, and not too modern. But down the street there is a bar built to the latest formulas and fashions: white walls, gray granite-topped tables and a loud, heavy beat blaring mercilessly from loudspeakers. In particular, it is the meeting place for young office workers.

Mary, my second wife, and I were in the habit of meeting at Lafitte—as we called the place—in summertime, after I had finished work on Fridays, some time between four and six, according to what was in the air and how the traffic behaved. In *summertime*, I write, but I should really say, the three summers we were married. In fact, I do not know where I ever got the notion of marrying her; perhaps it was for no other reason than to tease my children and their mother. I made a rule of calling her before I left the office for Lafitte, so she would not need to wait for me. As a result, we would always arrive at the same time. Sometimes I arrived a few minutes earlier, but never more than that. We always took the same table, looking out at the street. We drank cool drinks in the heat—I drank gin and tonic, she champagne tinted with cherry. Nothing eventful would ever happen, but we liked to sit sheltered from the hustle and bustle of the city and raise a glass to toast sunbeams or afternoon showers. She saw these outings as the start of the weekend, while I have never looked forward to days off work and therefore identified these moments only with peace and quiet and the drink, cool and bitter. Moreover, I was pleased to know there were fixed points in the swirling life of the city; I share with most people a delight in a certain stability and order.

As I have said, I recall nothing eventful from the times we spent at Lafitte, which is probably why I entertain such warm feelings toward the place. I did not sit down at my desk tonight to recall any major occurrences there; no, it was the bar down the street that suddenly entered my mind.

The summer before we got divorced, Mary repeatedly complained about aspects of our life. She nagged about Lafitte especially. "We must try something new," she said. The "new thing" was the place down the street; for some reason she was becoming more attracted to the noise there than to the quiet and stability which I sought. I absolutely refused to go there at first, told her not to dream that I would even set foot inside the door, that it was a zoo. When she continued pestering me, I restrained myself and decided to temporize and put off serious discussion of the idea. "Next time," I said when she phoned me at work on a Friday morning. "Let's think about it next week. I'm too tired to try anything new today."

My delaying tactics worked for some weeks, until eventually I could no longer manage to ward off her pestering. She had started to turn up late at Lafitte, her head hung low, and was sometimes rude to the waiter. She would even refer to the problem at crucial moments in our bedroom. And since the only pleasure I took in that woman was in the bedroom, I could do nothing but give way. I had to go.

I remember that day vividly. The sky was clear; it was not very humid, but comfortably warm, with a fine forecast for the weekend. The people at the office were in high spirits, entertaining their hopes of a pleasant evening and a bright weekend. I sent them all home at four o'clock, saying I did not like the idea of keeping them indoors on such a fine day. Myself, I stayed behind with my partner John Lazarus and put off phoning Mary, pretending not to have time to handle her nagging until six at the very earliest. I stuffed some tobacco into an old pipe I had kept in the top drawer of my desk ever since I stopped smoking twelve years before, put it in my mouth and relished the sense of the tobacco in the bowl, even though I did not light it. I arranged the papers on my desk, opened some letters and scanned the contents, placed a few of them in my secretary's file and tossed the rest into the wastebasket. Rushed nothing. Acted as if no one was hurrying me along. Every so often I looked out the window to watch the people pour out onto the street; there was excitement out there, and I regretted not being one of the group heading off quietly and peacefully to Lafitte. John popped his head into my office to ask why I had not left. After I told him what was keeping me back, he laughed and tried to console me, claiming I would surely be as fond of this new place as I was of my usual haunt. "We're too set to accept change without resisting," he said. "You can't teach an old dog new tricks."

The noisy, ponderous beat of music poured out onto the street as I alighted from the cab. Mary was waiting at the door, and I thought I could discern a triumphant smile on her lips. I remember telling myself while I paid the driver that she must be more stupid than I had imagined at first. It was crowded inside and we had to wait to find a seat.

"Fifteen minutes at the most," said a young man with fashionably styled hair, the back short and the top thicker. He swung one leg in time with the beat and asked if we would like a drink while we were waiting. In need of a gin and tonic, I drank from the glass without enjoying it.

Eventually, we were given a table halfway down the room, up against a wall. It was dark, with a cold breeze from the air-conditioning and with repeated disturbances from the rest room nearby and screeching from the loudspeakers right above our heads, somewhere below the rafters. My wife seemed to be enjoying herself; she wiggled in time with the music, smilingly watched the customers all around her (most of them were younger than my own children) and pointed out to me time and again how happy everyone seemed.

"Joie de vivre," Mary said. "It's such fun being among young people who enjoy life. Aren't you pleased you came? I don't regret it. Not at all."

She purred away like this while I remained silent. I did not know whether to feel anger or pity toward her: a woman of forty who imagined she could merge imperceptibly into a crowd of people in their early and mid-twenties. Gradually, her prattle began to go straight past me, for I was beginning to watch the gathering at the next table where a group of seven youngsters was sitting, two girls and five boys. None of them was older than thirty and the girls looked closer to twenty. There was no doubt that they were all colleagues at an office. The girls were wearing short dresses and high heels, a neat uniform but clearly not expensive. The males wore suits cut from reasonable cloth, nothing elaborate but serviceable all the same— clothes that no one would notice. For whatever reason, I could not take my eyes off those people until we left.

I remember everything as if it happened yesterday, for I understood much during those minutes that had been a mystery to me.

These people had first caught my attention when one of the lads asked the waitress to bring them a bottle of champagne and seven glasses. Clearly trying to impress, he not only asked for champagne but also specified the brand and vintage. Of course, I need not mention that it was not champagne but sparkling wine he ordered, a paltry brand and a meaningless vintage. Even though the thought of tasting that wine has never even entered my head, I knew instinctively that it had a sour bouquet, was green and immature, lacking all depth and register of taste, sharp to the tongue and harsh to swallow. But those people had no sense of what they were drinking: the girls squealed with glee and the lads puffed up like military commanders. They clinked glasses in a toast and repeatedly congratulated one of the girls, a brunette in a blue dress and white shoes who was neither plain nor attractive. "This is only the beginning for you!" "Congratulations!" "Fantastic!"

Listening more closely, I discovered that the girl had been promoted that morning. She was now assistant supervisor in the filing department. As far as I could make out, there were three employees in the department and she was now second in the pecking order, whether you looked at it from the top down or the bottom up. She had been working there for just over two years.

Their joy seemed all but boundless; the lad ordered another bottle of his soapsuds, they all laughed and screeched, told stories about their work. One of the girls, the secretary to the department manager, vowed to refuse to bring him coffee the following Monday; the other would put in a request in writing for a raise (she emphasized "in writing"); the lads planned to use their ingenuity and cunning to get themselves promoted from telephone salesmen to the much cushier job of traveling sales reps with company cars. They made fun of a handful of their colleagues and praised others: one was a skinny bitch, another kissed the sales manager's ass, but the switchboard receptionist was friendly and helpful. They talked about going to a disco later that night.

Sitting a few yards away from them in the cool breeze of the air-conditioning, I realized how trivial most people's lives are. What little difference it makes whether most people are born or die. If the girl who had been given a promotion were to have been run over by a car that evening and lost her life, her family would have mourned her, her friends would have missed her and her colleagues at the office would have asked, "Who's going to look after the files now?" But mourning wears off with time and the sense of loss likewise, and the assistant would be made assistant supervisor and another assistant would be appointed instead. He might decide to arrange all the legal papers in green folders instead of blue ones, and they would promptly go out to a restaurant to mark his reorganization program. And in old age he would boast to his grandchildren: "I was the one who had a new and better idea for arranging the company's legal papers." Perhaps he might try to remember other noteworthy events to recount to them: the day he married their grandmother, the morning when he bought her a washing machine, the night his son was born. "That's the way life is, kids," he would tell them, patting them on their heads. "A lot of things happen during a long life."

I watched them finish another bottle of sparkling wine. Tonight they are going to a disco, I said to myself, maybe grab some fried chicken at some cheap restaurant; one of the boys will manage to get one of the girls back to his place afterward, she will become pregnant, if not tonight, then the next time they go out. They will get married and he will buy her a washing machine. Half a century hence he will tell his young grandson: "It all started at a restaurant that closed down years ago. . . ."

I was feeling melancholy when Mary and I went out into the summer dusk; admittedly, the alcohol had impaired my perception of time enough to make our stay seem shorter than it actually was, but that revelation of triviality had saddened me. My children were unlikely to have any impact on the course of the world (I should be thankful if they went through life without major setbacks). Mary was stupid and vain at once, and my sole contribution to history was the little crime I had committed long ago. Nothing but that.

My appetite was dull and I was feeling tired, but Mary was in the highest of spirits. We went home and I fucked her in anger rather than passion. As far as I could tell, she did not notice any difference.

The day Father died I had a Chinese meal for supper. He had been ill for almost a week, and Mother phoned just after lunch to tell me he had died half an hour before. It was a Saturday and my wife and children were in our summer house. I did not need to look up the number when I phoned that Chinese takeout on Second Avenue to place my order, because I had done it so many times before. I named some dishes absentmindedly: chicken and broccoli in oyster sauce, sweet-and-sour pork, rice. Your meal will be ready in ten minutes, the girl said. As I put the phone down, I realized she had already hung up and said to myself that the Chinese who ran that place were polite and humble people, their food delicious and cheap to boot.

Did she say ten or fifteen minutes? I could not remember. It was well past eight. Ten minutes probably. They generally said ten minutes when it was getting on into the evening. I had not had the lights on, so I did not need to turn them off when I left my apartment. I had cried earlier in the day but no longer showed any signs of it, having rinsed my face with cold water. It was a humid, warm summer evening when your clothes stick to your skin. No one would even have noticed if my face had been swollen. One man's death changes nothing in the life of a big city: people walk the streets as usual, some rushing, others strolling, cabdrivers toot their horns, the subway trains come and go—the stifling heat they emit rises up through vents on the sidewalks. One man's death, another's birth, they change nothing.

I felt empty within, my thoughts fluttering and my feelings unclear. I had not seen Father for eleven years, since I moved to America, and did not talk to him often on the phone, rarely except at Christmas or when there was important news to tell. We had always got on well together, never harbored grudges against one another, but our relationship was still not close. I liked him. He was pleasant but secretive at the same time, methodical but light, a man of feeling who never let himself go, as they say. Maybe he became more bourgeois than ever after marrying my mother. I am not aware that he ever overstepped the bounds of the ordinary except when he frolicked with maids. I don't begrudge him that.

As usual, the food had been neatly packed in white paper cartons tidily arranged in a brown paper bag. I returned the greeting of the girl who served me. Inside, there was a strong smell of spices and sauces whose names I did not know. Outside were the street and sidewalk and at the back of the building only trash cans and alleyways, and the food was as good as the accoutrements of the place were modest. This unassuming takeout was a fixed point in my life, as Lafitte would become long afterward. Because I lacked roots, every sign of stability was desirable, however ordinary it might have been. All the same, I was fully aware that I had anchored my life in a way that would serve me well in calm times but not in storms. I was not prepared to X-ray my life and analyze my behavior at that moment, so I tried to empty my mind on the way home. I understood little, saw only an arm's length into the future, wondered at various aspects of my character, was sometimes uncertain of how I might react, yearned for things I could not identify. . . .

I ate the meal in the scant light in the kitchen, the chicken first and then the pork. I did not clean up afterward, but sat down in a chair in the lounge instead and stayed there until I fell asleep. It is not easy to distinguish my thoughts before I fell asleep from my dreams, for I slept lightly and my thoughts followed me into my dreams, and the dreams continued when I awakened with a start. The night passed between sleep and waking, memories and dreams, truth and fiction, affirmations and doubts. I woke up from a game of football on the meadow by the church, fell asleep in my old bed with a Tarzan comic open beside me, stared out of the east window of our summer cottage by Lake Thingvallavatn. The Tarzan comic faded and I lit a cigarette: it was a week since I had gotten home from Denmark, my little crime behind me. The lights go out in his window, you are inside, you whom I loved. I woke with a start, my heart pumping as I raced home to the room I rented, my legs like lead. Father led me by the hand around the lake, tickling my palm with his thumb: there was our house in the pure light of morning. And there he was with the maid in his office—or was it him? Wasn't it me? And you on the sofa, you with your skirt hitched up, beckoning me to come to you. . . . An uneasy night.

Shortly before dawn I awoke and went to the bathroom for a shave. I turned on the light and toyed at length at wetting the shaving brush and twirling it around the soap to make a great thick foam. I spread it over my face and shaved carefully. Exhausted after that night, I perked up somewhat after the shave. When I had finished in the bathroom, I noticed the daylight trickling into the apartment past the curtains, through a tiny chink by the window frames. The aftershave nipped my skin; I had shaved too close.

I had promised Mother I would take the first plane back. She was not taking it well. This was the first time I thought of her as being old.

I feared the journey home.

Nothing had changed inside the house, everything was in its place. The same carpets on the floor, the same pictures on the walls, and the grandfather clock in the sitting room measured the time as it always had, its ticking punctuating the monotone of silence. Nothing had changed except Mother: she had grown much older during those eleven years. I put my bags in the guest room, hung up my shirts and suit in the wardrobe, arranged my socks and underwear in the two top drawers of the dresser, laid down the magazines I had brought with me flat on top of some books on the bookshelf. My room would be too small for me now, Mother said, the bed was too narrow and there was all sorts of rubbish in the cupboards as well.

At first I felt as though I had never left. Father could have been at work, or taking a walk or at a meeting of the anglers' club. I sat down in a chair in the sitting room, fondled his pipe and matchbox, read the paper and drank coffee, and even thought I could hear him walking up the steps to the front door. It was not until evening, when I lay down to rest, that I realized that everything had changed. The silence was not the same as before and other feet walked the carpets, other eyes looked at the pictures, and the chair in the sitting room where Father always used to sit was vacant. His pipe was empty and there was no smell of tobacco in the air. I got out of bed at three in the morning; it was beginning to get light and I had grown unaccustomed to the bright Icelandic summer nights. The clothes he used to wear had been arranged in his office: his black trousers were folded over the settee, there was a pile of white shirts on the desk and two pairs of shoes on the chair. It was as if someone had begun to move his clothes out of the bedroom and down to the study, but stopped halfway through, had forgotten about it or perhaps had second thoughts. The coy daylight crept in through the window, over the suspenders on the back of the chair and the pants on the settee, over the pen on the desk and the inkwell beside it. It was then that I realized that he was gone and would never return; no one would ever wear those shirts and his shoes would never again be polished; what I had wanted to say to him—explanations of my silences and my absence—I now could never say. So much was left unsaid, even though we had always gotten along well together. Our conversations had been short, sometimes telegraphic:

"Everything okay, Pete?"

"Everything's fine; Gudrún's well. Helgi too."

"And business?"

"Fine."

"Is there anything I can do for you?"

"No, I have everything I need. Thanks all the same, Father."

"Maybe you'll come and visit us soon? It would be nice to meet your wife. And your children—we still haven't seen them yet."

"As soon as we have the chance, Father. I have so much on my plate. You know how it is. The company's still young. You know how it is when you start out."

"Let me know if there's anything I can help you with. Don't hesitate to let me know."

"You'll be the first to know. Thanks, Father. I'll let you know."

"We could go fishing together."

"Have you caught anything recently?"

"I went to Sog a month ago. Caught two salmon and a trout."

"What about Thingvallavatn?"

"I fish there when we go to the cabin. Your mother has had the flu lately, so we haven't been there for three weekends now. I bagged a lot the last time I was there. Did handsomely."

"It would be fun to go fishing with you, Father."

"Yes, you'd enjoy it."

"Sure would."

"Give my regards to your family, Pete."

"I will. And good fishing this summer."

That is what our conversations were like. I laid the bow tie on a shirt on the desk, folded the pants better over the settee, took the cap off the fountain pen and, taking a fresh sheet of paper, reminded myself how smooth it was, and comfortable to hold. Father used to sit down for a few minutes in the evenings and scribble in his diary with it before he went to bed. No earth-shattering news, just a report on the weather and everyday events: bridge results in the winter, the outcome of his fishing trips in the summer. I pulled out the bottom drawer and found the little notebook he had been using as a diary: 1 FEBRUARY 1951, he had written on the flyleaf. More than three weeks had passed since his last entry. Absentmindedly, I thumbed through it until I caught sight of my name in a passage under the heading 20 DECEMBER.

"Christmas preparations are in full swing," it said. "Lovely weather. Cold but still and clear. Spoke to Pétur today. He won't be coming back for Christmas, as we had been hoping. It's been a long time since I have seen him. Somehow Christmas feels half-empty to us without him. I hope he is getting along well. . . ."

I read those words over and again, until they started to echo in my head. "Somehow Christmas feels half-empty to us without him." Why didn't you ever tell me, Father? Why did you never ask me to come back? I should have sensed it. You shouldn't have had to ask. I should have sensed it in your voice, how happy you were when I mentioned I might be coming back for Christmas. Of course I should have sensed how you were feeling. I did, but paid no heed. Why was I mentioning going home for Christmas before being certain that I would? It was just an idea I had one Thursday afternoon. By Friday it had vanished from my mind. But Father did not know that, and immediately began looking forward to welcoming us. For months he looked forward to seeing me again. Imagine his disappointment when he phoned me on December 20 and I told him I was unable to get away from the office. I had all but forgotten ever mentioning the possibility of a Christmas visit to him.

"Maybe next Christmas," I said. "I can't get away now. You know how it is when you're starting out."

"Oh well, Pete. That's the way it will have to be, I suppose. I hope you and your family have a Merry Christmas. Let's at least phone each other on Christmas Eve."

How could I have been so inconsiderate? Eleven years. I leafed through other notebooks that I found in the drawer: MARCH 1942—DECEMBER 1943; MAY 1945—NOVEMBER 1946, etc. I was frequently mentioned: they seemed to miss me more than I could ever have imagined.

"Celebrations today. Pétur and his wife had a son this morning. Six pounds eight ounces. Strong as an ox, Pétur said when we spoke to him on the phone. Will he take after his father? How nice it would be to see him. I hope it will be soon. . . ."

How could I have done that to him? Eleven years. How could I. . . . "Good fishing today. Reminded me of the time Pétur and I went to the lake in '30 and '31." "I read in the papers that there is a heat wave in New York at the moment. I hope Pétur and his family are not feeling the effects too badly." "Perhaps Pétur will come home this summer. I have been thinking of buying plane tickets for his family and mailing them over, but have abandoned the idea. Maybe they would think I was interfering. . . ." How could I. . . .

The tears streamed down my cheeks uncontrollably. I hid my face in my hands and covered my mouth with a handkerchief so that my sobbing would not wake Mother. "Dad. . . ." Outside, dawn broke as I still sat in the chair. My body continued to shake long after I had stopped crying. I could hear a thrush singing nearby and watched the gnats buzzing against the windowpane.

Why did everything have to turn out like this?

On bright mornings, when everything is lit and nothing is hidden, the mind finds it hard to fill in the blanks of shadows. I prefer twilight, an unfinished tale, a compromise between darkness and light.

We were sitting in the kitchen, a few minutes past eight o'clock. I had awakened early to the singing of birds and the brightness; the curtains in the guest room were too translucent and I was still unaccustomed to the bed. Mother made coffee. My sister Disa had just come in. She lived on the east side of town; I had never visited her and her husband. It was a Wednesday.

"Have you spoken to the minister, Disa?"

"I spoke to him on Sunday. It's all settled."

"Who's the minister?" I asked.

"An old school friend of Father's, Bodvar Gunnlaugsson. Father had said Bodvar should preside at his funeral. The last time he mentioned it was last Christmas, to Mother."

"Your father liked Bodvar. Said he was never—what was it he was never, Disa?"

"Pretentious or sanctimonious."

"That's what he called it. I remember now."

"Where's his parish?" I asked.

"Somewhere in the countryside."

"Your father wanted a simple funeral."

"It will be a modest affair, Mother."

"But I'll still need to serve the guests coffee afterward. And pastries too."

"We'll see to that. Don't you worry about it."

"And mow the lawn. The grass has grown too long."

My sister had grown prettier over the years. She had always been attractive, but time had been kind to her: she had grown unquestionably prettier.

"You're looking good, Disa."

"Thanks. It's been a long time since we last saw each other."

"You know how it is when you're trying to make a go of things. Time flies."

I wanted to avoid the subject. Wanted very much to avoid it.

Mother came back from the sitting room. "When is the minister due, Disa?"

"After lunch. Half past one."

"Are you sure you spoke to the minister?"

"Yes, Mother. I'm certain."

"Half past one," she repeated three times. "I must tidy up before he arrives. Do you think he will have had breakfast by then?"

"She's showing her age," I said when I could hear her already upstairs.

"A lot of things change over eleven years."

I put sugar into my coffee and stirred it.

"Is she in good health?"

"She's old. But there's nothing particularly wrong with

her. High blood pressure, that's all. Father's death affected her more than she lets on. I still don't think she's faced it."

"Is she going to stay here?"

"We haven't discussed that yet. Perhaps she could move in with us. We have plenty of room."

"Do you trust her to live on her own?"

"I don't know. She always had a maid to help her, but that's all changed now."

I realized for the first time that there was no maid in the house.

"She hasn't had a maid for three years. Not since Bertha died. Do you remember her?"

I nodded. Of course I remembered her. They took her on about two years before I left for Denmark. I suspected that Mother had chosen her because of her age. She was past fifty when she started working in their home. Perhaps Mother suspected Father was fooling around with the girls. It would not have surprised me.

"I didn't know she was dead."

The minister turned up after lunch. I thought he was moved by Father's death, which surprised me. I had thought most clergymen regarded bereavements as commonplace occurrences governed by incontrovertible laws beyond human understanding and action. He asked the necessary questions, clearing his throat from time to time, seemed patently uncomfortable and appeared relieved when he picked up his coat and walking stick and left. In God we trust, I said to myself. A harmless old duffer, even though I have never felt warmth toward the agents of God, who have always reminded me of shifty businessmen.

After dinner we sat outside in the garden. The sun was still high in the sky and some boys were playing football on the lawn down by the lake. I had opened a bottle of cognac that I found in the cupboard and Disa and I were drinking it in the evening calm.

"Father used to talk about you a lot, Pete."

I said nothing.

"He was proud of your success. There are two of you who run the company, aren't there?"

I said yes and told her about my partnership with John Lazarus.

"Did he ever mail you any plane tickets?"

"What?"

"He spent years wondering if he ought to send you and your family some tickets to Iceland. As a present. He was beginning to miss you. Maybe he thought it would have been interfering. That's why he never went through with it."

We sat in silence for a while. An occasional breeze ruffled the leaves of the trees, and shadows flickered on the table between us.

"I miss him, Disa. I should have. . . . "

We finished the bottle in the garden. Mother was taking a nap in the sitting room after dinner. I draped a blanket over her. Disa decided to stay the night, and just past eleven o'clock we said goodnight to each other. When we went to close the back door, she said as if talking to herself: "Strange thing, Pete. Father claimed more than once to me that you had changed after staying in Copenhagen. Something must have happened, he said. Otherwise he wouldn't have changed so quickly. It's funny how we sometimes appear to our parents. Maybe we know as little about them as they do about us. Goodnight, Pete."

The cabin was located among some shrubs down by the river. Frissi pointed it out to me shortly before we reached the bridge: a white cabin with a green roof.

He had approached me while we were standing outside the cathedral the day before, waiting for the hearse to drive away. Frissi was unchanged, apart from being fatter. Over coffee after the ceremony he invited me on a fishing trip to Sog.

"I must show you the cabin I bought in the woods there last year. And the whiskey bottles I keep in it."

"Your friend Frissi is really making a name for himself," Disa told me. "He's amassed franchises for everything you can think of. Sure works hard."

At first I hesitated to accept his invitation, not thinking it was proper to leave Mother alone at that time, but told myself that she had Disa and furthermore might even want to be left in peace.

"It'll do you good to be outdoors," Frissi said.

He drove fast and the dust whirled up in a long cloud behind us. Benign puffs of cloud were in the blue sky; the sun broke through intermittently to shine on the calm river. Father was always warning me about wading too deep in it when I went on fishing trips with him as a boy, because the current is deceptively strong and there are slippery stones on the riverbed. We generally fished up-river from the bridge, but I still recall casting farther down also, at the confluence of Sog and Hvita. I visualized my father and myself on the riverbank as we drove over the bridge, saw us clearly as if I were an unfamiliar traveler passing through one district after another and had noticed this tall man with his son by sheer coincidence. He was wearing a green raincoat and was bending over to help the boy change a fly. "This is the way, big man," he was saying. "This is the way, Pete. Twist the yarn between your thumb and index finger and thread the end through the loop. That's the way, yes. . . ." I could see it all so clearly.

The trail leading to the cabin reached most of the way to the river. It ended in a clearing close by the cabin and we got out and stretched our legs. A few sheep that had slipped through the fence rose and ambled away from us. The shadows on the face of Mount Ingolfsfjall were darker than I had remembered and the silence that engulfed us was more profound than I was prepared for: no rush of cars, no shouts, no clamor. I stood still for a while inhaling the scent of heather and shrub. I also thought I could detect the smell of sheep, even though they were out of sight by now. The car engine emitted a crackling sound: Frissi had been driving fast.

"Nothing ever changes here, Pete. Let's lug the stuff out of the car and indoors."

I had felt uncomfortable on the way out of town and was on the point of asking him to turn back when we passed the hill just on the outskirts. I could envisage Mother alone in the house. Perhaps she would be sitting in Father's office looking at his books on the shelves and the pen on the desk, the pants on the settee, recalling old times and remembering how soft his hands were. She would be thinking about them, imagining them, then suddenly feel him stroking her cheek. With a start, she would realize there was no one there, only her sense of loss that she was buckling under, and she would lean over beneath its weight and hide her face in her hands. The good years behind her and the times beginning that she always said . . . and I was far away, I had not seen her for eleven years but left town when she needed me, rushed off on a fool's errand. I was leaving the country after a week. Would I ever see her again?

Inside the cabin was the same smell I remembered from our cabin on the shores of Lake Thingvallavatn: a mixture of rot and damp. The smell of no one there, Father used to call it. Cans of food in a cupboard, blankets on benches in the bedroom, an oil stove in the sitting room. Frissi talked; I listened distractedly and nodded or grunted in agreement every now and then. We sat by the window and drank coffee braced with whiskey. On the opposite bank of the river, there were people making hay; I watched them glide across the meadow as if in a silent movie. The whirring of the tractor did not reach me either, and the barking dog could not be heard. I knew that by all rights I should have been feeling good in such a place, but I was still uneasy and apprehensive, sometimes on edge, without knowing why. When the sun had passed behind the mountain and its shadows were growing darker, we went out to try some fishing. I watched the shadows gliding across the people in the meadow, and felt for an instant that I was calming down.

"I'm going upstream," said Frissi. "Don't you want to take the hip flask with you?"

I walked along the riverbank, my rod in my left hand and a can of worms in my right, made my way along the dirt trail and concentrated on not tripping over the rocks or branches that lay over it. A car crossed the bridge below, and it was so quiet all around that I could hear the passengers singing inside. Then everything fell silent except for the enchanting murmur of the river and the whoosh of shrubbery as I made my way through it.

"You should try using a fly, Pete," Father said. "It takes some skill, fly-fishing."

"But I only have a worm with me," I answered instinctively.

The murmur of the river, it must have been that. His voice was so clear—as if he were standing by my side. It must have been my lack of sleep and the murmur of the river.

"I'm going to see Mother tomorrow," I said. "I'll leave in the morning. The moment I wake up. I always meant to come back home long ago. You know how it is when. . . ."

The worm vanished into the water; the current carried the line downstream, I could not see where.

"You were right, Father. Something did happen in Copenhagen."

"The bed's slippery, Pete. You should be careful."

I stepped into the water; it was chilly.

"Got one!" I heard Frissi shout.

I was wearing knee-length boots, but did not realize I had waded too far out until it was too late. My boots were full of water and the cold gripped my feet.

"Wouldn't it be fun if we could go on a fishing trip in the summer, Pete."

"I doubt whether I'll make it back, Father. You know

how it is when you're trying to make a go of things for yourself. . . ."

"Ten pounds at least!" Frissi shouted.

"The stones on the bed are slippery. You should be careful," Father said.

I could not feel the riverbed, but kept on wading out all the same. The water reached halfway up my thighs, cold and dark.

"There's a heavy current," Father said.

Those voices, those voices . . . I could hear them all at once, unable to tell them apart. My rod slipped out of my hands. The current snatched it away downstream.

"Be careful, Pétur!"

"A ten-pounder! Maybe fifteen even!"

"He said you'd changed after staying in Copenhagen."

"The ship is leaving tomorrow morning. Let's meet at the harbor at eight o'clock. There must be no delays." Leaving tomorrow, my little crime accomplished. . . .

The ceaseless murmur of the water, the voices, the merciless current. I was unable to move, no longer knew where I was, staring into the darkness of the river. I did not come to my senses until I heard my name.

"Pete? What's wrong? Do you need some help?"

Frissi had walked downstream and was standing on the bank where I had left the can of worms.

"Pete, is anything wrong?"

"No. I just dropped my rod."

"I can't hear you, Pete. Do you need any help?"

I turned around and inched my way toward land. Father was right: the current was strong and it was difficult to keep your footing on the bed. I took a long time to wade ashore, and when I clambered up to the bank, my teeth were starting to chatter and my feet were numb.

"What happened?"

"I dropped my rod. Slipped on a rock. The current's strong."

"But you were just standing there. You didn't move. Just stood there."

"I couldn't move in that current. It was too slippery. Did you catch anything?"

He told me about the salmon he had landed.

"Cognac?"

He had taken the hip flask with him. We drank from it. I could not feel my toes.

"Are you sure you're okay?"

"Positive."

He told me to go into the cabin to get warm while he went to collect the salmon he had left on the bank up-stream.

I looked at the mountain and the town at its foot. A light was burning by a front door. To the east there was a slight glow in the clouds. Calm. Quiet. Peace. A curlew chirping in the fen on the other side of the river. I did not go into the cabin; I walked to Frissi's car, sat behind the wheel and drove away.

I knew I would never be coming back. I knew I would never return to Iceland.

The flies were dancing on the windowpane. When I looked out through the window at the endless flatness of Denmark, I could not help missing the mountains in the vicinity of Reykjavik—Esja, Skardsheidi, even the Oskjuhlid hill. But here—not a rolling foothill in the summer mist, nowhere a mountain in the clear daylight of winter. Flatness, nothing but flatness, as far as the eye could see.

My landlady was flustered one morning when she woke me.

"The Germans have occupied Denmark!" she blurted out, standing in the doorway. "They invaded us this morning while we were asleep."

"While we were asleep"— would it really have made any difference whether we were awake? I was unable to discern either fear or joy in her voice; more than anything else she reminded me of the newspaper boys who always stood on the corner by the Reykjavik Pharmacy shouting out the headlines with more zeal than understanding. She had rushed out to the street before I could rub the sleep out of my eyes, either to the baker or the butcher or to the grocery store, the main meeting places in the quarter.

Two days have passed since this happened, and I still have not heard a gun fired. I have seen people talking surreptitiously against walls and pointing out unwelcome guests in uniform on the other side of the street with glances or quick nods, but heard nothing of conflicts or any resistance. I would go so far as to say that life is proceeding normally: the German soldiers are thanking their lucky stars for having been sent to Denmark, where no one has tried to resist them and there is delicious ham on fresh bread to go with a glass of beer. I looked out the window and told myself that the Danes were dancing to the Germans' tune just like the flies on the windowpane, and the resistance they offered was in total accord with the flatness of their country. How could we Icelanders have allowed this puny nation to push us around for centuries?

The last time I met you was on the eve of the occupation. We went to the movies together; you enjoyed yourself more than I did on that occasion. I knew where you were going afterward, even though I gave no indication and behaved just as if everything were in order, as if I did not even suspect his existence. When I walked you to the station, I did not return home, but hid instead in a nook by the entrance, behind a pillar by the newspaper racks to be precise. I admit that I gloated as I waited for you: I could feel my power; I had the upper hand and was able to watch your every movement without your suspecting a thing. You strode away determinedly to meet him, no need for you to wait very long after I had left. There was expectation in your movements. I acted cautiously and kept a considerable distance at first, then quickened my pace, for you looked neither left nor right as you walked along, and least of all behind you. You went straight into the house where he lived, without looking around before you entered, with no need to worry about me: of course, I had gone home and gone to bed or picked up a book to read—I certainly had plenty of boring books to chose from. He had been expecting you and let you in immediately. I waited outside in the street, leaned up against a wall as usual and lit a cigarette—this was not the first time I had followed you here. When the lights in the window went out, I did not fall to pieces as I had done the first time but contemplated how I might take revenge. For weeks I had been racking my brains wondering what kind of revenge would not only make you regret deluding me and acting like a slut but would also make you beg me for mercy, make you repeat, sniveling, morning and evening, day and night: "What can I do to make you forgive me? What can I do? I'll do anything . . . anything. . . ." The words jangled in my head on the way home, like the lyrics of a catchy song; I envisaged you groveling at my feet in pain and regret, as if I were watching a movie projected on a screen. "Isn't it a bit late for whimpering now?" I would say. "Wouldn't it have been wiser to have considered the consequences earlier?"

As on a screen, I mentally acted out the scene over and over again, always enjoying it, always feeling better after the show. I thought it more convenient, however, in these fantasies to forget that it still remained completely unclear how I could take my vengeance.

Now, half a century later, sitting here in the light at my desk, an old man, my body sick and my spirit weary, now the most natural reaction for me would be to smile to myself at these recollections and say (silently at least) how amusing it is to think what a fool I was at that time. I should have engraved in my memory the expressions on people's faces and their conversations the day their country was occupied, German movements through the streets of the city and the news of bloody struggles coming in from

Norway; I should have forgotten everything but the war and ignored my own trivial problems that had no bearing on the fate of the world. Instead, I was thinking about you all my waking hours, ignoring the great events going on right outside my window.

That was the way I was thinking during these days, the way I remember. This will never change. Providence blessed me with an opportunity for vengeance so terrible that I can never see those times in their true light.

Drizzle at the most, I had said to myself on the way, as I felt the first drops on my cheeks. I cut a slice of rabbit and watched the rain pouring in streams down the windowpane and over the name of the establishment. My fellow Icelanders turned up one after another. You were right when you had predicted it would be crowded that night. Sitting at the table next to us were laborers who had just left work; their shoes dusty, pleasantly fatigued after a long day's work. Thinking about them now, I wonder how long it has been since I have been able to enjoy a relaxed evening after physical exertion, taking it easy after a hot bath, sitting in a chair with a book in my hand and the knowledge that my sleep will be deep and peaceful, then waking to gratifying aches in the morning. A long time indeed.

You introduced me to people I had not met before. Most of them were university students; a few others were youths who were working in Copenhagen. Besides them, there were some others who seemed simply to be killing time. You introduced me to him hurriedly, not lingering but rushing away from the table to greet a girl you had seen through the window on her way in.

"Jon, Pétur, Pétur, Jon," you blurted out.

We shook hands. I tried to tell from his expression

whether he knew about me, gave him a good, long, straight look in the eye. He was taller than I was—an inch or two at least—stocky and sloppily dressed, clearly on purpose. His pants were not pressed, his sweater baggy, his collar undone. I was surprised that he was not smarter.

"Been here long?" he asked.

"This winter. And you?"

"My first winter too. You were at the high school, weren't you?"

"I went to business school to please my dad. But that's all behind me now. I'm studying history."

"I'm taking courses in economics and accounting."

"Really."

This expert in world history who was beginning to learn the art of deductive reasoning was clearly not impressed.

"But I do read a lot of philosophy and history, for my own pleasure," I added.

Why am I trying to impress him? I asked myself. Why try to please him?

"Pétur, this is my friend Dadi Kristinsson. Pétur's studying accountancy. Maybe you recognize him from high school?"

And then he started talking to you and I to Dadi Kristinsson, who had been two years my senior in high school. I cut another slice of rabbit and drank some beer. It was still raining. There was some talk that it would be a rainy summer, but I thought such forecasts were on the hasty side.

Toward nine o'clock everyone who had been expected had turned up. Those who had been mingling sat down at the table and the rest of us moved along to make room for the others. Most of us drank beer; the others who had not eaten ordered cold meat or sandwiches. I knew the meat was a better choice than the sandwiches but kept this to myself, not wanting to draw attention to myself and also feeling that some of them probably could not afford the meat.

Gradually, the group began to settle down, and everyone who had been laughing and joking suddenly remembered that the occasion of this gathering was deadly serious and merriment was out of the question. The girls hid their smiles and stopped their bantering, the males frowned and drank their beer slowly and methodically as if tasting it for the first time or mentally trying to solve a complex mathematical problem. People started looking over toward Jon with expectant expressions. He fell silent momentarily, then began talking, slowly and statesmanlike. I could easily have believed that Jon had been rehearsing; how naive of me to believe he was genuine, speaking so brazenly in a public place.

"We must do something," he said. "There's a war going on. Some thought Hitler would draw the line at Poland and Czechoslovakia. They were too optimistic. I am certain this will be a long war. Some of you will obviously want to get back to Iceland. I wish you a good trip. But finding passage on a ship won't be easy."

"We've contacted the embassy . . ." a couple in the group began, but Jon raised his hand immediately to show that he knew all about it and needed no details.

"They will stop at nothing," he continued. "Don't imagine they would be so polite and indifferent if the Danes had resisted. Everything would be different. I've heard they're acting like barbarians in Norway. They've dropped their masks there. Here they don't need to. Not yet.

"As far as I see it, this is the situation: if I were to go home, I'd go back to my room with Mom and Dad, go out dancing on weekends again and probably try to find myself some kind of job for the time being. I'd be ignoring what's happening in the rest of the world. My life wouldn't revolve around freedom or slavery, life or death, but around whether I could find a decent party to go to on Saturday night or what movie was showing on Sunday. Nothing else would matter. I'd read about the war in the papers and wait for enough people to sacrifice their lives until everything returned to normal and I could come back here to finish my studies. Of course, I can well understand those of you who want to go back home. I wish you a good trip."

He fell silent and looked around the group. No one said a word, some of them looked the other way; nobody dared to mention returning home. Myself, I deliberately grinned a half-grin when he looked in my direction. I could see his disapproval.

"Those of you who are planning to go home really ought not to stay here any longer tonight. Those of us who are staying need to talk. We need to decide how to act in German-occupied territory. There are only two options: do nothing, or resist."

He lowered his voice: "An underground resistance movement is being mobilized. I've had the good fortune to meet some of the members. A well-organized movement to work against those animals as best they can. There's no question that it will be a large and powerful movement.

There aren't many of us Icelanders here, but we can make a contribution. I offer to put anyone here who is interested in contact with the resistance movement."

Having finished his address, he leaned back in his seat. We all exchanged glances and began whispering. He was bombarded with questions: What action was the resistance going to take? How many members did it have? Where were its headquarters? Did the Germans know about it? and the like. He gave no answers, adopted a pensive, cryptic expression, hinted that we would have to decide our next move before he would contact his "friends" from the resistance movement.

"Think over what I've been saying. There's no need to make any decisions tonight. Sleep on it."

We sat there until past eleven o'clock. Then the gathering broke up and we set off outdoors one after another, into the rain that by now had turned to drizzle. You stayed behind with him, and I could not bring myself to chase after you. I had no doubt where you were going to spend the night. When would you if not tonight, after the address by the hero of the resistance? I flirted with your girlfriend on the way out, but you did not notice.

It continued to rain well into the night, and I lay unable to sleep, watching the darkness play across the hat I had hung up to dry on a peg on the door.

I have heard voices saying; Come! I have heard voices saying; Go! Yet I remain motionless, for I do not know where to go: every journey must have an end.

I have not seen my children since the funeral, but I do not miss them. I am astonished by their behavior. Helgi lets his sister push him around; it is amazing how that boy has amounted to so little. The summer is passing like all others, autumn is near and then winter—and spring? I forecast a cold winter.

The images haunted me again last night. The body was more disfigured than usual this time: blood dripping from the corners of the mouth, the skin so white that it shone. I awoke exhausted; the gentle breeze rippling the curtains was too warm to be refreshing. At dawn I dressed, took the elevator downstairs and told the boy, the doorman, to go out into the street and hail a cab for me. I suspect I woke him up: it was before six o'clock. Sleeping on the job, I thought to myself: you can't trust those East Europeans. And I pay more than enough for their service.

This was not the first time I had traveled by cab around the city in the early hours of the morning; no, I make a habit of it. Whenever the daylight is gray and the streets are empty, before the sun rises and the streets are filled with ants. I told the driver to go down Fifth Avenue. Beneath the eastern wall of the Park, there were homeless people sleeping on the benches; most of them had bags and cardboard boxes by their sides, some had been lucky enough to acquire a share in a grocery cart. I told the driver to drive slowly; empty cabs rushed past us in search of passengers, but there were none to be had so early in the morning. I know that some people find the metropolis a lonely place at this time, before it comes to life, but I like it best then. One man is opening the door to his store, arranging the fruit outside, turning on the lights. A baker puts his loaves in the oven. Gulls fly in the direction of the East River. A child tosses and turns in its bed behind some curtains.

We ended down in the meatpacking district, where the occasional figure was up and about hosing down the sidewalks and yards, then headed back up west of the Park, up to Seventy-ninth Street where my son Helgi lives. I do not know why I told the lad to drive there; perhaps I wanted to recall the facades of the houses in his neighborhood, since it was a long time since I had seen them. No one about and the lights of the apartment were turned off; perhaps he was on vacation. I admit I longed to see his face, even though it had always lacked definition—vague and vacuous: the face of a man who will have no impact on the world. Yet I still have my hopes . . . a sign of old age.

I have doubtless been too lax with him, pampered him. If he had been through everything I have had to put up with, he might have been a different person. If he had had to fight for every penny, outwit everyone who wanted to swindle him (there has been no lack of such encounters in my case), he might have acquired a tough edge. I remember the way their mother treated me sometimes, when she pretended to have heard about my business practices. It's easy enough for people who have never had to get their hands dirty to pass judgment on the rest of us. If I had not bought those shares in Scandinavian Imports, someone else would have. Of course, I bought out the company when it was in trouble and the shares were reasonably priced. And what choice did I have but to fire the previous owner once I had made the deal? So what if he had founded Scandinavian Imports many years before? How had he been running it? Why was it on the verge of bankruptcy? I deny that I had anything to do with the slump in the share price before I bought my way in. No one could claim me responsible unless he was jealous of me. You can listen to them for as long as you like. You can fill your heads with lies and slanders, whispers and speculations. They know nothing! They ought to show you their bank statements. Don't they look a bit on the lean side? Actions speak louder than words, I have always said. Bullshit and slander bounce off me. I am immune to defamation. Otherwise I would have been dead long ago.

Some people even claim I bribed the old man's former financial director, John Lazarus, to cook the books. Some people say I rewarded his dishonesty by giving him a share of the company after I bought it. Slander, I say, nothing but defamation. But their mother believed these stories. I could never forgive her for that. Neither did I enjoy selling the apartment that was included in the deal. I found that tough. But I needed cash to pay my debts and it was not my fault that the old man's daughter had to move out as a result. Should I have given her the apartment and let the company collapse again? Tell me: what would you have done in my place? Don't imagine I sold the roof over her head for my own private amusement. Don't imagine that for an instant! It hurt me. But that's life. Sometimes you have to do what you have to do. I took on the old man and won. That's all there was to it. Don't you think he would have enjoyed the chance to throw me out in the gutter?

Helgi—he has never had to make an effort for anything. His mother spoiled him from an early age and I was too lax with him. Wouldn't he have been tougher if he had had to live even a single hour of my life? Wouldn't he have been taken aback to come home in the evening and hear accusations from his own wife, snide questions and insinuations of dishonesty? You need strong nerves in this life, strong nerves and determination. Otherwise you lose. I am saddened by the thought that they will squander my money after my death, even though they will only receive a tiny part of it. What fun it would be to have children who could gladden my old age, children I could be proud of.

We drove homeward, south of the Park and up Madison. At Sherry-Lehmann they were selling futures of '89 Bordeaux. A promising vintage, but the wines are still a good ten years away from maturity. I pondered the advertisement in the window. Strange to think that I would never be able to enjoy those wines.

Sitting in my chair last night, I wondered whether I should bring my discussion of slander and defamation to a close, but concluded that I could not. There are so many rumors that they demand explanation; time is short and I alone can distinguish between truth and lie, calmly and knowledgeably.

I should mention from the outset that I am not ashamed of my business practices. Far from it: I am proud of them. Yet I have had to undertake many tasks through necessity rather than for pleasure. I know more about the rumors than you think. I know not only what is rooted in truth and in fabrication but also nearly all spinoffs of the fabrications, because I always kept track of the gossip. I was quick to realize that the people who pretended to be my friends were no better than the rest; this did not upset me—I grew accustomed to it early on. Often I relished listening to the stories. It was like sitting in an auditorium in the dark, watching a show: I could see everything, hear everything, and nobody was aware of my presence. Besides which, the actors upon that stage were playing me. What a treat!

The gossip from November 1967 is still fresh in my memory. It was early in the month, shortly before the onslaught of winter, and the weather was still warm if I remember correctly. This gossip began when I had clinched a franchise that someone else had held for a long time, a lucrative and secure franchise. I had made a verbal agreement with the owners of the Swiss company at the time, to be followed by a written agreement that December. Though I say so myself, I displayed exceptional management talent in the fight for that franchise. I was like a grandmaster at a chessboard, at once resourceful, controlled and unfathomable. I foresaw my opponent's every move but concealed my own strategies, disguised rooks as bishops, knights as pawns, advanced, never retreating, advanced relentlessly. Foresaw it all—ten moves ahead, twenty moves—saw everything and relished every moment of the conflict. But the details are too numerous for me to dwell on; I shall merely commit to paper a few of them that bear upon the origin of the gossip.

When I ask myself what gave me the upper hand in that brawl, I hardly need to rack my brains very long. Herr Metzenauer, the managing director of the Swiss company, had decided to spend his vacation (or part of it at least) in New York the summer before. I clearly remember that he arrived on a Friday, and his wife and three children on Sunday. He had rejected in advance all overtures from myself and my rival (whom I shall call Mr. A.) since he planned to spend his vacation in the bosom of his family, far from all business concerns.

For some time I had been putting out feelers to learn as much as I could about Herr Metzenauer, what sort of character I was dealing with. I discovered that he was strict but honest, religious, and a churchgoer, a sworn enemy of drink and tobacco. The reports I received about him emphasized his intolerance of hedonism and irresponsibility. Uptight, I said to myself when I finished reading the reports. My plan was complete. It came to mind without the slightest warning, without the slightest effort.

It was simple: I knew Herr Metzenauer would be tired after his long trip from Switzerland and would therefore dine early and go to bed no later than eleven o'clock. He was staying at a hotel on the south side of the Park, and through not too ingenious means I found out, before he arrived, which room he would be given. I thought him most likely to dine at the hotel, but for safety's sake I posted someone in the lobby to watch his movements in case he decided to take a stroll in the warm dusk to catch a bite elsewhere. He was supposed to let me know when Herr Metzenauer returned to his room after his meal.

Everything went like clockwork. Herr Metzenauer checked into his hotel at five o'clock, stayed in room 1527 until seven, then went out for a brief constitutional. Returning at quarter to eight, he was seated at a table in the hotel's best restaurant at eight o'clock. He began with a bowl of soup with which he drank soda water, then it was on to duck for his main course, with a glass of nonalcoholic wine. After dining he sat in a deep leather armchair in the lounge, drinking coffee instead of cognac and browsing through a copy of *Die Welt*, which he had either bought at the hotel or brought over from Europe. At twenty minutes to ten he rose to his feet and took the elevator up to the fifteenth floor, well fed, tired, and ready for bed. Two minutes later my collaborator phoned from the lobby and said, "He's gone up to his room."

"Action," I said. "Send the girl up."

All I regret is not being able to see the dear old boy's face when he answered the door. In fact, he did not open it straightaway but asked for her credentials.

"A present from Mr. A.," she answered.

Then he opened the door; she said good evening, unbuttoned her coat and stood in front of him, a Negress wearing nothing but her panties.

"Mr. A. was worried you might be lonely tonight," she said. "He asked me to keep you entertained."

She told me later that this must have been the first time Herr Metzenauer had ever met a woman of her profession. He blushed and stood motionless in the doorway, fumbling for words for a while, looking at her as if he had never seen hips and thighs and breasts before in his life. When he finally snapped back to his senses, he said hurriedly: "Just go back home, my dear. There's nothing for you to do here."

Delighted, the girl took the elevator and said she had never earned her fee with so little effort; I turned off the lights in my office and went home triumphantly.

On Sunday morning, when his wife and children arrived, I sent a bouquet of flowers to her and a letter to him. In the letter I began by welcoming them to the city, then enumerated the churches I thought he might wish to visit (you can never trust hotel staff for that sort of advice, I wrote). Furthermore, I mentioned the districts that were inadvisable to visit at night and warned him of others that should be equally avoided in broad daylight. In addition, I included the names and telephone numbers of various reliable restaurants and said I hoped his family would be able to enjoy their trip and not be bothered with business and customers. If there was anything I could do for him, he should not hesitate to get in touch with me. Yours sincerely, Peter Peterson.

The day before they left, Herr Metzenauer phoned to thank me for the letter and my consideration. The family appeared to have followed my directions as if they were the Ten Commandments. I wished them a pleasant journey home and said I hoped to be meeting them shortly.

I had no fear that he would mention the girl's visit to Mr. A. and thereby discover the hoax. He was far too discreet for that. Undoubtedly, he would think it best to remain silent about Mr. A.'s miscalculation.

Toward autumn, stories began to circulate. I was trying to wrest the franchise from Mr. A., people were saying. I had flown to Switzerland four times, they said; three trips in September and one in October. Keeping myself busy all right! According to my sources, Mr. A. still remained hopeful and denied all the rumors, saying that as far as he knew all my hustling had been in vain. "You can trust the Swiss," he said confidently. "I've enjoyed good cooperation with them. They have no reason to make any changes here."

It was not until November, when Herr Metzenauer informed both Mr. A. and myself of his decision, that the gossip became torrential. Mr. A. took his loss of the franchise badly, held forth about dishonesty whenever he started drinking and harangued people with diatribes about my character, on which he seemed to have very firm opinions. I ignored this, but when I discovered by chance that he was going out to a restaurant one evening, I paid someone to sit at the adjoining table so that I might receive a precise account of his state of mind. I did this purely for pleasure, since by this stage I had already floored my opponent and only formalities remained to be settled.

Mr. A. was well behaved before his meal, drank his whiskey in silence and left the chattering to his companions. There were four of them in all. It was not until they had gotten through their dessert, along with two bottles of white wine, that his tongue began to loosen. I shall not repeat in detail what he said about me—you can imagine the gist; it's enough to reveal an allegation he made that was to spread during the following weeks and opened the way for the slanders. As I recall, it went along the following lines: "He must have paid some whore to go and lay that bastard Metzenauer and had them photographed. Then he must have threatened to send the pictures to his wife and the board of directors. Wouldn't surprise me, guys. Wouldn't surprise me."

Of course, this was nothing but talk and Mr. A. naturally forgot his words the moment they left his mouth. But somehow, stories got around. Long stories and short ones, well told and badly told, in laughing or shocked tones, countless stories. They were whispered at the coat check in the concert hall, in front of the mirror in the rest room where the ladies were putting on their lipstick during the intermission, over the urinals where their husbands stood with their flies undone.

"Rented an apartment for him and a woman to go with it. Then got the whole thing on tape."

"Shows it to his friends at his house."

"Not all of them though."

"Only the closest ones."

"You don't say!"

"He's a weasel."

"Cunning bastard."

"Invited that Austrian around and showed him the skin flick. Threatened to send the tape to his old lady."

"Would stop at nothing."

"Offered him a bowl of popcorn while he showed him the films."

"Popcorn?"

"A bowl?"

"He's always been like that."

"So what's A. going to do?"

"A.? What can he do? He's finished."

"Haven't seen the film, have you?"

"Not me."

"Neither have I."

"Christ, it'd be something. It'd be fun to see that film."

So, by sheer chance, the slander had a bit of truth to it. But this is of course the exception to the rule, which is probably why I recall our battle over Herr Metzenauer so well. I admit it warms my old heart to think about it. To my astonishment I realize, as I am about to put down the pen, that I wrote this chapter with a smile on my face, so it seems appropriate to enjoy opening a good bottle of red wine before the clock strikes seven.

I stand up and tell myself on my way to the cellar that there was once a time when no one was a match for me. No one at all.

There was no war going on in the B. Andersen & Sons bookstore. It was as peaceful as ever, the same scent of coffee, the pastries hot, with their soft sugar coating. The printed word held its ground: no one entertained the idea of removing from the shelves any books that the new authorities might have disliked. By day, customers roamed up and down the stairs, took books from the shelves and paid for them downstairs, and other copies were put in their place. In the evenings there were still readings and sometimes music recitals. I went there regularly as before, possibly more often, and bought more books than would have been advisable according to the laws of accountancy. I had had the good fortune to receive a check from home just before the country was occupied.

As far as I could see, business was booming by day, and in the evenings the Germans joined the throng listening to the readings, young men who sat at the back of the room and kept to themselves. I thought they would have preferred to be out of uniform, dressed like everyone else, undesignated, lovers of literature and music. Many of them had a good grasp of Scandinavian languages, some spoke fluent Danish and others appeared to understand it. Works were sometimes read in English and French, and B. Andersen or his sons had the sense to give a higher profile than before to German culture, by, for example, bringing in singers of lieder by Schubert and Schumann and others of their kin.

I do not remember how it came about that I started talking to Andreas Klotz. He was my senior by a year, and had been studying classics when the war broke out. Polite and agreeable, completely free of boorishness or bossiness, he was well read and easy to get on with. He visited B. Andersen & Sons when he could manage it; I doubt whether he went there less than once a week.

You had stopped going there with me, saying you would prefer me taking you to the movies or to a pub to meet other people, so I went on my own and had to like it. And as time went by I looked forward to meeting Andreas Klotz in the bookstore, enjoyed discussing topics with him that few of my compatriots were interested in and that were beyond the comprehension of my fellow students at business school. We sometimes swapped books; I would have had nothing to remember him by apart from a volume of Schiller's verse on my bookshelf had Providence not intervened. We spoke of the serious things in life, as young men often tend to do; he even started talking about the war once we had gotten to know each other better.

"The unification of Europe," I remember him saying. "French and Scandinavian literature, German music, Italian art. Isn't it about time we supported each other? I respect the nations that Germany is at war with now. I hope the war is nothing more than a stormy courtship. It's what follows that is important. Marriage—that's what everything is about. . . . I thank God I'm here and not somewhere else."

This was the tone of our conversations at the B. An-

dersen & Sons bookstore, young men full of optimism—
straightforward and naive. We never walked together after
the gatherings or met at other times, never bade each other
farewell at the door or said goodnight. He made a habit of
not putting on his cap until he was some distance from the
store; I thought that was a considerate gesture, since the
cap completed his uniform, and without it he was to some
extent a civilian like the rest of us.

"Pawns like us. We have as much say in all of this as
you. I just hope this is nothing more than a stormy
courtship. . . . It's starting to rain. Better be off now. See
you soon. *Gute Nacht.*"

I walked home, solemn and pensive, for I had for all in-
tents and purposes reached an agreement with the powers
that be that the war was nothing more than a lovers' tiff. I
had not suspected, when this took place, that Andreas
Klotz could help me take my revenge.

I ought not to put it down in writing. I have never told anyone about it before, and it is unnecessary to reveal it to anyone now. I ought to be able to laugh at these memoirs, if everything were in order, but instead I am embarrassed when my thoughts turn to those days. Those minutes, to be more precise. I have always envied people who have the knack for describing their youthful selves in the third person, as if their pasts are no longer any of their business. This is why I am upset at recalling my trip to the Vesterbro quarter—not on moral grounds (I have long since stopped worrying about such things) but because of how humiliating the journey turned out to be.

I went there because of you. I had stood too many times outside in the street (up against a wall, away from the streetlights) while you allowed him to pull the curtains, hold you and enjoy you. Stood there like a fool, tormenting myself with mental images like a voyeur at your window, watching your lovemaking. Myself, I had never been with a woman. I did not know the rules of the game and was terrified by the unknown. I hated you and yearned for you at the same time, yearned to spend my life in your company; sometimes I became wild with rage but crazed with yearning at the same time, and did not know which was which, could not think a single thought through.

Worry gnawed at me when I realized I would make an idiot of myself if I ever did spend the night with you. I could imagine you either laughing at me or smiling pityingly. *He* knew what to do, *he* was as confident as an ace pilot flying blind. I lay awake at night, poring over my ignorance, sometimes needing to reach out and light a cigarette in order to restore my calm and my conviction that there were things I could do competently. I would exhale the smoke through my nostrils or blow rings, twiddling the cigarette between my fingers and blindly knocking the ash into a tray on my bedside table.

But smoking was of little avail, so one day I decided to go to the Vesterbro. I bought a bottle of liquor on the way home from school and drank a few glasses that evening to get my courage up before setting off. I had had little to eat and the alcohol went to my head sooner than I had expected. I had heard of a certain house there that distinguished itself in the quality of the service it provided. Some of my fellow students had visited such institutions and in class the following day would compare the services provided. I listened to their conversations and memorized the details, even though I never asked any questions and pretended I was uninterested in their chitchat.

It was a wet and blustery evening when I walked the short distance down to Strøget, with a theme in my head from a recital at the bookstore a few days before:

> *Ich such im Schnee vergebens*
> *Nach ihrer Tritte Spur,*

I warbled to myself, my intoxication rendering me indifferent to the cold.

Wo sie an meinem Arme
Durchstrich die grüne Flur.

But there was no snow on the streets and therefore no tracks in them; only the howling of the wind and litter swirling around my feet. People were sitting over hot meals and wine or coffee in cafés, talking about the weather and complaining of the cold, saying how they hoped it would warm up again soon. Germans were walking the streets in twos and threes, the wind was blowing and I quickened my pace, head bowed to avoid being recognized. I was nearing my destination and wanted to play it safe in case any of my fellow students were in the quarter. Or you. For some peculiar reason, I was half afraid of bumping into you. What would I answer when you asked where I was going? What could I say? But naturally I met neither you nor my fellow students that evening.

On Vesterbro there were four scroungers playing trumpets and begging money, but on Helgolandsgade the only music was the sound of old standards through a half-open window. I hurried past people on the street and darted into the house I had heard them talking about the instant I caught sight of the number above the door. The stairs creaked as I went up; there was the stench of beer and sweat, but I did not turn back. When I reached the landing, I was greeted by a man who looked to be in his forties, balding and fat and wearing a dirty white undershirt. He looked at me, said nothing, lit a cigar butt, exhaled the smoke and looked at the cigar as if to measure how many more drags he could take without burning himself. Then he looked back at me and said curtly; "Have you been here before?"

I shook my head.

"So you don't know the rules of the house?"

I shook my head again.

"Got any money? It ain't for free."

I told him I had enough money.

"How do you know what's enough?"

I braced myself, cleared my throat and told him I knew how much I was prepared to spend.

He smiled. "You know that, do you? You sure seem to know a lot." He took another suck on his cigar butt, knocked the ash to the floor, then looked at the smoke and named a figure that I thought was exorbitant.

"That much?"

He rubbed his left hand dreamily over his unshaven chin. "There are soldiers in town," he said eventually. "There's more demand. You interested or not?"

I said I was.

"Pay me now. Tip the girl afterward."

I took my wallet out and counted out the notes. He put his cigar butt in his mouth while he counted them; I was certain it would burn his lips, but it did not.

"It ain't for free, you know. There are soldiers in town," he muttered and gestured me to follow him up the stairs.

I followed him down a dim corridor until we reached door number five, which he opened, saying, "Behave yourself, now. Remember, I'm downstairs."

I asked if I had a choice, recalling that my fellow students said you could choose for yourself.

"Any one in particular?"

I did not know any of their names, not having memorized them if I had ever heard them at all.

"There's not much choice," he said. "You have to take what you get. There are soldiers in town."

Before closing the door, he turned around. "Wait here. She'll be along."

The room was cold and the windows were steamed up. The only furniture was a bed and a dressing table with a mirror on the wall above it. The bed looked wobbly to me, but I sat on the edge.

I was startled when she came in a few minutes later. She opened the door firmly, but closed it gently. I stood up. She was around my age, big and plump, with a red sheen to her hair. She was wearing a red dressing gown.

"My name's Bibi."

Not knowing what to say, I merely nodded.

"What's your name? Surely you have a name?"

"Pétur."

She sat down on the bed and patted the mattress to show that I was supposed to sit down beside her.

"Where are you from?"

I was about to tell her when it dawned on me that some of my classmates might also be her customers. She might tell them.

"I'm from the Faroe Islands."

"Got a girlfriend there?"

"No."

"Here then?"

I stared into my lap. "Maybe."

"Maybe? That's a bit rough."

She seemed to me now to be younger than me, a year or two, perhaps three. That disturbed me. I would have preferred an older woman—thirty, maybe even thirty-three.

"Have you ever been here before?"

"No."

She looked at me, and I looked at the wall in front of me. I could tell she knew, tell exactly when she realized that I had never been with a woman before.

"Then you don't know the rules of the house. We don't have much time. Get undressed."

I stood up and took off my jacket. She lay down and undid her gown; I could see her naked body out of the corner of my eye, her big white breasts and ample hips, her long legs. Then she raised her knees, moved her legs apart, began stroking herself and said in a different voice, "Come on."

I took off my sweater and shirt and kicked off my shoes, but got no further, because she pulled me down toward her, unbuttoned my pants and pulled them down. Before I knew it, I was between her legs and thrusting away as if to the beat of a hidden drum.

"Oh yes," she said. "Oh, oh. . . ."

The drumbeat grew faster, her breasts shook, white and big, faster. A spasm seized me, my body shook. "Oh," she said, "oh, oh. . . ." Then everything fell quiet.

I got up and pulled up my pants, put on my shirt and sweater and jacket, laced up my shoes. She ran her hand through her hair and wrapped the dressing gown about herself. There was no question she was at least two years younger than I was. It had not taken long. She watched me dressing without speaking.

"So that's that, then," she said at last.

I reached into my pocket and took out my wallet, but before I had time to count out some money for her, she said: "You don't need to pay me for that. I'll get my share downstairs. It was nothing."

Nothing! I felt the blood rushing to my cheeks. How could she. . . . What did she mean? Nothing. . . .

I do not remember whether I said goodbye to her when I opened the door and crept out into the corridor and down the stairs, do not remember whether I said anything to her.

"Do come back!" she called out after me.

He was standing in the same place on the landing as when I had arrived but had stopped smoking his cigar butt.

"Wow, finished already?"

Instead of answering, I dashed down the stairs, threw open the front door, ran into the night, fleeing my humiliation.

When asked, as I often am, about my contact with other Icelanders in New York, I have always avoided answering. Before I begin to feel drowsy again in my soft armchair beneath the dull light of the lamp, I want to try to remember the circumstances under which my dealings with them came to an end—abruptly, it seems.

My arm has been numb today—my right arm, to be precise—and I have been resting. I believe it is a Thursday but am not certain and cannot be bothered to stand up and go find out for sure. My arm numb, other parts of my body too, my thoughts apathetic, no fear of death. But this might well change tomorrow.

The first year after I arrived in America, we Icelanders would always meet at the Viking bar. Some of us went there every day, some every other day, and very few only once a week. It was invariably a merry gathering, although it sometimes had its serious sides too. Those of us who worked as buyers for wholesalers back in Iceland used to compare prices and quality, payments and credit, but without revealing anything to our competitors. We did not say much about tampering with the waybills, except for the odd idiot who had drunk too much. I remember clearly that the slickest operators could manage to declare only one-tenth of their consignments without getting collared by the authorities back home. Hannes and I took a careful approach and rarely made good with more than a quarter. These were the swashbuckling days of a new age of prosperity, of work for the taking and mortal dangers.

I avoided thinking about my little crime, avoided it entirely; it was not until later that the images began to haunt me. We were in a new world; old sins could be forgotten.

Looking back and reflecting calmly on the course of events, I find it only natural that I should have lost those acquaintances I made the first year. We became too closely attached, met too often, talked too candidly, knew too much about each other. As time went by, it would have taken only a minor incident to create lasting discord. Now I no longer wonder at it, but feel that everything followed its expected course. Only the breach in my friendship with Hannes might have been avoided.

Somehow Hannes and I managed to sleep with the same girl two days apart. Not on purpose, if my memory serves me correctly. Admittedly, he would sometimes claim later that I had done it to tease him, or that we had a bet which of us could get her into bed. Exaggerations, even though I admit that we both spent the night with her: Hannes first; I two days later. Such was not unheard of in those times of booming business and work for the taking. We rushed all over town by day, negotiating lower prices and more goods, went down to the ships, in and out of banks, from one office to the next, always bursting with energy and knowing that opportunities were countless. In the evenings this energy was impossible to turn off like water from a tap; oh no, we went on making conquests and charmed many a woman, young lads with blood racing through our veins. What could be more natural than for two friends to end up with the same woman?

The whole matter would have been done with had she not phoned Hannes a few weeks later to announce that she was pregnant.

"She's absolutely set on having the baby," Hannes said that evening over a bowl of soup at the Viking bar.

"Didn't you try to talk her out of it?"

"Hopeless."

"Couldn't it be someone else's instead of yours?"

He looked at me with a sarcastic grin. "Yours."

"No one except us?"

"No."

"Do you believe her?"

"Why shouldn't I?"

He seemed rather curt when I suggested the possibility that someone else could have been the child's father.

"Didn't you use a condom?" he asked.

"Of course I did. Didn't you?"

"What do you think?" But then he added: "She couldn't remember if you used a condom. Said she'd had too much to drink that night."

If the truth be told, I could not remember either, because I had had a few too many that night as well. However, I did not see the need to tell him.

"She doesn't have to remember," I said. "I remember."

We parted.

Two weeks went by in which we did not speak to each other. Not only had I been busy in the meantime, but we were still bothered by that conversation at the Viking. The girl, on the other hand, phoned me three times during those weeks. She was a decent type, really, but not exactly with much upstairs; after her third call I had convinced her that she clearly remembered that I used a condom on that fateful night. In addition, I insinuated that Hannes might perhaps have ridden bareback, as the saying goes. I promised her I would make sure that the child would be provided for.

"I'll handle Hannes," I said. "Don't you worry about a thing."

The next time I met Hannes was at a party given by a mutual friend. At first we did not mention the pregnancy, but later Hannes took me aside.

"Have you been getting at that girl?" he asked. "Now she says she's not sure if I used a condom when I was with her, but swears that you did. Don't you think that's a little strange?"

"The last time we talked, I told you she was nuts. You should have believed me."

I could tell that he did not trust me.

"We must be able to find a way out of this mess," I said. "There's no need to make a big thing of it. Your wife—"

"She must never hear a word about this! Not a word!"

"Take it easy. Of course she'll never hear anything."

Someone passed us on his way to the kitchen, and we fell momentarily silent.

"You're still single, Pete. What if you admit it's yours and we'll split the maintenance fifty-fifty? I don't think there's a fairer solution."

"Surely you don't expect me to admit paternity of your child, Hannes."

"My child."

"Your child. She says she remembers me using a condom, but not you. Still, I'm prepared to make sure your wife never hears a word about it."

Of course, this was just boyishness on my part. There was rivalry in the air. He threatened me before storming out the door, abused me, but was aware at the same time that I had won. He was fond of his wife and children, was always talking about them, wrote to them regularly, kept photographs of them in the American fashion. He was looking forward to going back to Iceland and did not want to risk anything.

He must have confided in someone about his predicament, because the slanders and backbiting soon began. Everyone took his side, everyone except two or three who bore him old grudges anyway. But I did not trust them either, so their support was worthless. The Icelanders stopped inviting me to their parties; I became a pariah, a rogue whom no one dared associate with. I could not have cared less, since I had grown bored with those people I had seen every day or every week for a whole year. I had listened to them telling the same jokes a hundred sixty-seven times and wasted my time bullshitting with them about things that I could not even remember when I woke up the next morning. I was given the cold shoulder at the Viking and ceased going there; after all, the food had not been anything to write home about, and there was nothing I would miss from the ignorant and petit bourgeois wine list. Hannes discreetly admitted paternity and made sure the mother had enough money to feed and clothe the child. But it didn't cost him much, since the girl got married when their son was just a year old, and her husband never wanted to see either Hannes or his money. He was completely off the hook.

Hannes went back to Iceland without saying goodbye to me in 1944. I never had any more contact with the other Icelanders who stayed behind. I would go so far as to say that those people (I have no hesitation in saying this) are like Icelandic wholesalers: uncultured and vain, lazy, unimaginative and pampered. None of them was possessed of more than average intelligence and none of them could stand the strain of making money: the girls turned into old women overnight and spent their time arguing about which of them had a prettier dress or larger apartment; the males grew soft and flabby, their faces ruddy from prosperity, but invariably half sheepish, like most of my compatriots who do business in another country. They became far too satisfied with their lot too early on, all of them grew too worldly before they realized what the world had up its sleeve. Nobody gets very far who allows word to get around that he is interested in money for money's sake. Indifference on the surface and toughness underneath: that's what counts. And knowledge of higher things. Lofty thoughts.

I do not miss them. Do not miss anything from that time. God forbid that I should ever meet their ilk in the next life—which I do not believe in anyway.

After that I began to dislike him. Obviously, I had a grudge against him before, but it was still you I blamed. I assumed he knew nothing of our relationship and thought it likely that you were using him in the same way as you were using me. It was you I intended to get even with, and my vengeance (whatever form it would eventually take) would be directed against you, although I would not be able to avoid punishing him as well. You had stopped seeing me, stopped noticing me. When we went out together, you pretended to listen to me but did not hear; your thoughts were elsewhere (I knew where) and you spent more and more nights with him.

What excuse did you give to the people you were staying with? That you were staying with your girlfriend from Iceland? That struck me as most probable and I suspected one girl in particular of complicity in your scheme. Because you gained control over people, attracted them to you: whether they wanted to or not, they developed a fondness for you. And you took advantage of that mercilessly.

Dislike him, I write, but I ought to be more explicit: after that, I began to hate him. The expression in his eyes that day, his grin, the sarcasm in his voice: he knew what he was doing and relished it. He was no pawn in your hands.

You were far away when it happened, because it was purely by chance that our paths crossed. I had nipped into the foyer of a restaurant in Strøget for some lemonade in the heat, sat down on a stool while I was drinking it and did not expect to see anyone. There were two of them together and they noticed me from the street; I could not remember the other one's name—Björn, perhaps, or was his surname Björnsson? It does not matter. They came in to greet me, ordered a beer and complained of the heat as they mopped the sweat from their brows. The clock struck two, I remember that clearly. I disliked the tone of his voice, even when he was talking about the weather; there was something behind it, I could tell. The one whose name I had forgotten said little and was clearly nothing more than a convenient sidekick.

As I was about to take my leave, Jon said: "Has the accounting department thought over what we were talking about last time?"

"What?"

"The last time we all met."

I pretended not to get the point, so his buddy reminded me, grandiosely.

"Maybe you've been too busy to devote any time to this," said Jon.

"We always talk about so much when we meet," I said. "I'd forgotten all about it."

"This is one issue you can't forget."

I agreed.

"Are you in?"

I answered to the effect that I needed to think it over before making up my mind. "Have many of the others joined?" I asked.

"That's nobody's business but their own."

"No, of course not."

A pause. Not thinking it would be right to leave then, I ordered another glass of lemonade.

"Are there perhaps better things to keep one occupied at business school?" he asked snidely as his companion smirked. "Perhaps there's so much womanizing going on that there is little time for world affairs. Perhaps people have forgotten there's a war on. Perhaps they don't notice the Nazis in town."

His buddy had stopped grinning and was staring goofily ahead, rubbing his index finger along the handle of his beer glass. Don't lose your temper, I told myself; let his words vanish into thin air.

"Perhaps it might interest the boys in business school to know that there are men around who can service women and the world at the same time. Service women as well as anyone else can."

"Really," I said.

"Do you reckon there'll be many women left for the boys in business school when it's all over? Denmark and Norway fallen, the Netherlands and Belgium. Who can tell how long the French will hold out? Maybe there won't be any women left for the boys from the accounting department when it's all over. Just bear that in mind and do what you plan with those women before it's too late."

Those women. So he knew, he took delight in letting me know that he knew. Keep your cool, don't let him make you lose your temper. . . .

"So how many Germans has the hero of the liberation chased out of Denmark?" I asked.

"What we do in the resistance is none of your business."

"It looks as if you have plenty of time to drink beer and take things easy though."

"You'll never do anything that takes guts. . . ."

"Come on," said his buddy. "It's useless."

They stood up.

"I hope you don't splash too much blood all over yourself," I said.

Instead of delivering more abuse, he settled for a smirk. "Happy hunting, lover boy."

They left and I remained behind, my lemonade no longer cold and refreshing. I had a queasy feeling in my stomach and my head was abuzz. He had amused himself by mocking me, called me impotent. She must have told him I had not yet slept with her. I could imagine them lying there together talking about me.

"He asks me out to the movies."

"And holds your hand."

"Says I love you."

"Then says goodnight."

The curtain had risen before my eyes, my inadequacy revealed, my weakness detailed, my emotions mocked. I would bring them to their knees. In the rush of my thoughts, in my agitation, my little crime kindled. I was terrified when the idea occurred to me; fear and horror beset me—and contentment at the same instant. Could I bring myself to do it? I asked myself. Could I? Fear and anguish and delight excited my body.

Could I bring myself to do it?

All your vainglorious days have passed. In a fraction of a second they have passed. And then, it is as if you had never existed at all.

I tried thinking of a place where there would be few people about in the evening and I could be sure we would not be seen. I contemplated one place after another and finally decided to arrange a meeting with him on the other side of the Knippelsbro bridge, by the old warehouse down from Strandgade. The buildings were empty at night and so were the streets, with scant lighting outdoors and the houses as dark as black cliffs.

I phoned him.

"I must meet you," I said. "I want to join the resistance. We must meet alone. Promise not to tell anyone."

Jon promised.

Nothing could have been more natural. The Germans were starting to execute members of the resistance, leaving their bodies lying around to be seen. No witnesses. Only vacant eyes in cold, rigid bodies found the next morning. I took the gun from my bedside table and gripped it with my right hand: it fitted my palm well, felt suited to my grip, my index finger touched the trigger at precisely the right place. Andreas Klotz had not noticed when I removed it from his holster, felt nothing amid the crowd at the B. Andersen & Sons bookstore the previous evening. Nothing could have been more natural: a young man from the resistance movement found dead at daybreak one Saturday when the laborers turned up for work. Lying in a pool of blood, shot straight through the heart. The autopsy would reveal that the bullet was from a German pistol.

I took a cab. Wanting to get there before him, I set off early. We had arranged to meet at ten o'clock. It was raining and overcast, steady rain, neither drizzle nor a downpour. I was wearing a gray overcoat. When the cabdriver spoke to me on the way, I did not reply, because I could not hear what he was saying, did not listen, had only one thing on my mind. The gun felt cold in my pocket: when I gripped it, a curious sense of contentment rippled through me. I told the driver to stop by the Knippelsbro; I would walk over the bridge myself.

I walked slowly. The buildings grew closer through the lasting rain: cart depots, stables, peat stores and the big warehouse. There were deep striations in the sidewalk marked by the iron frame of the cartwheels, heavy planks boarding the doors of the storehouses and iron bars over the windows of the office annex. The smell of sea and tar and canvas and wet timber.

I walked over the Knippelsbro with only one thought in mind: would I recross it as a murderer?

The girl went out early this morning and has yet to return. I cannot understand it; it is four o'clock. I have just phoned the doorman downstairs, but he is useless as usual.

"She left before nine."

I told him I knew that; I was not asking when she left, but whether she had come back. They never understand, those Latins. The money I pay for the service! She is not in the habit of going out without letting me know when she will be back. Yet I do not recall her telling me this morning when she would return. I cannot remember it, so it is out of the question that she ever mentioned it.

I look out of the north window and scan the street for her. Then I go into the kitchen and look south. Fruitless. Or is it? Isn't that her on the other side of the street, on a black bike? No, the gray car-exhaust fumes fooled me: it was a boy, Chinese in all probability, making a delivery from the takeout.

Left before nine and has not been in touch. Half past four now. Something must have happened to her. She might have fallen off her bike. Or been knocked down by a car. I have tried repeatedly to persuade her to throw that wreck away, but those Orientals are stubborn. They are different from us. She is obedient, but obstinate as a mule all the same. She cannot have been hit by a car, otherwise the hospital would have phoned me. She has no one but me, so I would have been the one they alerted. I cannot understand it.

Everything in the kitchen is spic and span: the dish-cloths are hanging in their place, the soap is by the side of the sink and there are no dirty dishes waiting to be washed (she never leaves dirty dishes in the sink). More to the point, there is even some tea in the yellow thermos and coffee in the red one that she must have prepared before she left. Everything as it always is, nothing out of place.

Before she left! She can't have left me! I refuse to believe it! I run into her bedroom, open her wardrobe and pull out the drawers, but since I do not know what is usually there anyway, I cannot tell whether anything is missing. There are not many garments in the wardrobe, but who knows, it might be all she owns. I have never noticed exactly what she wears, never made it my business.

She can't have left—she must not! I shall give her dresses and blouses and pants and sweaters when she comes back. I shall spare no expense, simply order her to fill her wardrobe, with no ifs, ands or buts. Money's no object, I shall tell her. Money does not matter to me anymore. I have plenty, more than I can spend myself. Pretty blouses and sweaters, not items on sale; she must go to quality stores to buy those clothes, quality stores where the staff will pamper her. Perhaps I'll go with her to make sure she is given first-class service. Maybe I shall do that for her, who knows? Then I shall put on a white shirt, wear my summery blue suit, a yellow bow tie with blue spots, put a handkerchief in my pocket and slip on some white shoes. Put on a white hat with a blue band. Maybe I shall do that for her, who knows?

But I must decide on the total before I take her shopping. For no other reason than to let her know in advance how much she may spend. Otherwise it will be a fiasco. It has always been vital to me to know beforehand how much I am going to pay. I have never been impulsive in money matters. "Just pay later," people would sometimes say, "don't worry about this trifle. We'll square matters later." But I would demand to know the price, to hear it from their lips, to register it in my mind. I have never forgotten a single sum of money, never let myself be caught off my guard in business. You should have known me when I was younger. Everything I touched turned to money. Opportunities never slipped through my hands, they multiplied. I loved making money, loved to know that my name was all over it in banks and brokerage houses. At first I made a habit of taking money home with me every so often so that I could count the notes, feel them. This is what I have earned with my own brains and hands. This is *my* money. No one can take it away from me.

My first wife knew of this obsession of mine and disliked it. She suspected me of being unable to resist the temptation of a quick profit, wherever and however. But she never understood me. I would never have entertained the idea of doing anything dubious, never even thought of breaking the law. Then I could have lost everything. I always liked money too much to play for ultimate stakes.

"We don't need all that money," she would often say. "We can get by on less."

To her credit, she never squandered money. She spent

it wisely and never let people cheat her. The first year we were married, I gave her an allowance every week, but when I saw that she knew how to manage money, I decided to do this on a monthly basis instead. Such a shame that she failed to instill the same frugality in our children. Sometimes I think it would be a good thing for them not to get a cent from me. Yet they expect me to hand over the fruits of my toil on a silver platter. Here, help yourselves. Go on, please squander everything I have earned during my lifetime. Thank you. I am delighted you will oblige. . . .

Surely she could not have gone to see them? Six o'clock and she is still not back. Could they have gotten her to meet them somewhere? At Helgi's place, maybe? That could not be—sitting around her like vultures, interrogating her.

"What does he put all his money into? Is it in the stock market? Or real estate? Does he spend anything on himself? Hope he's not giving it all away to outsiders. Money that's ours by rights. Never could trust him. Never could . . . does he talk about us? Does he ever mention us? What does he say? What . . . ?"

Those unspeakable layabouts. I cannot believe she has gone to meet with them. She would not. She knows how I feel about them. What could she hope to gain from that? Unless they promised her a share of the inheritance. Unless they convinced her I was not going to leave her anything.

"We'll take care of you, if you help us. . . ."

No, they are not smart enough to think like that. Lack imagination. Their brains are numb. Their minds slack. Their hands do not know what it is like to grip and wrestle. She could not possibly be with them.

Where is she? I phone the doorman downstairs again, but he has not seen or heard anything since this morning. Says his name is Axel. I think the other one is called that too. Maybe they are all called Axel and sleep when they ought to be working. Hear nothing and see nothing.

I turn on the light in my study, because it is beginning to get dark. Clouds fill the sky; there will be a thunderstorm tonight. It has grown more humid and the heat would be unbearable if I did not have air-conditioning in the apartment. Anticipating a downpour, people are rushing to finish their business, trotting along the sidewalks, wary of the lull before the storm. Where is she?

I balk at the thought she might be gone. I have no one but her. Strange to come to the end of your life this way: a girl from a country I do not know, the daughter of a couple whose whereabouts are unknown to me, lives in my home. By chance, sheer coincidence. If she leaves me, I shall have no one. My children . . . I have said enough about them. They are just testimony to a mistake.

She must come back. Please do not leave me. Do not turn your back on me when there is so little time left. I shall do anything for you. If you want money, take it. If I can do anything for you, name it. Don't hesitate! Don't leave me behind in the twilight. Soon the lightning and thunder and rain will be here. The images in my mind as night falls.

S he did not come back until dark. Half past nine. "Where have you been?"

"At a wedding. I took the train at nine this morning. Don't you remember? You should have come with me. It was fun."

Suddenly, I remembered. The wedding of John Lazarus's ex-secretary somewhere out of town, a petit bourgeois wedding with all the trimmings. In America people sometimes spend as much as two years on wedding preparations; the marriage seldom lasts that long.

"I was beginning to worry about you. You should have let me know. At least you could have phoned me to tell me when you were getting back. I haven't even eaten supper yet."

"Don't you remember that originally I had planned to stay the night there? But then you asked me to come back tonight and I said, 'I'll be back late, maybe not until midnight.' 'Just as long as you come back tonight,' you said. Have you forgotten?"

Our conversation the previous evening had completely slipped my mind, but once she jogged my memory, I remembered every single word.

"Of course I hadn't forgotten. But I don't want you

roaming about at night after dark. How did you get back from the station?"

"I walked."

"How many times have I told you to take a cab at night? It's not surprising I was worried."

"Cabs are a waste of money."

"Why worry about that? Besides, you need to get yourself some new clothes."

I had rarely heard her talk so much at once; it was clear my forgetfulness perturbed her. Was it her care for me that broke her silence? Curious, that silent dignity . . . that can only be molded in suffering and fear, on the battlefield, in war, between brothers. She has never told me about growing up in Cambodia, never mentioned the carnage. But I have read about it. What tragedy! What a mess!

That silent dignity . . . it stared me in the face one September evening last year and did not yield an inch. Perhaps I might have drunk too much that evening. I was fitter then than I am now and had been visiting with an acquaintance of mine. I have known him for a long time; he is an importer of French wines and has always been there for me when I have been rushed to find a rare bottle at a decent price. Not intending to stay with him for long, I had the driver wait outside for me. I remember the car was black—a Cadillac in all probability. Anyway, he made more of my visit than I would ever have expected, and I stayed there several hours longer than I had planned. I had to try the Pauillac and the other Graves. "I've been waiting to taste this wine with someone who appreciates it. Wonderful, don't you think? A fine structure . . . like strata in the earth . . . like the layers of a cake!" Had to compare vintages. Vertical tasting; horizontal tasting. We were not in the best of shape when we clambered up the stairs from the cellar and parted with a bear hug at the door.

The driver was asleep in the front seat; I woke him up and told him to drive around the streets awhile instead of taking me straight home. To begin with we crawled along the narrow streets of Little Italy, where people were sitting at tables on the sidewalks, telling stories or talking about the summer that was coming to an end or whispering something no one else was supposed to hear. Then we headed along the west side of the Park, cruised around and took things easy. The street life had a pleasant effect on me, the energy and pace, the spectrum and languages, the noise and calm, the beauty and ugliness. I could feel life coursing through my veins, power and yearning in my body; I was not a decrepit old man but part of the eternal energy of the metropolis.

She had gone into her bedroom when I returned home. I had been thinking it over on the way, planning how it should be. For the moment had arrived, there was no mistaking that. I had clenched my fists repeatedly in the backseat of the car, and I felt my strength growing instead of dwindling each time. I did not turn on the light but went straight to the bathroom adjoining my bedroom, undressed and rinsed my face with cold water, washed my arms and chest and stomach. I stared at myself in the mirror: it was a long time since I had seen such purposefulness in my face. There was still strength in those muscles, my heart pumped blood and my nerves went taut with an unambiguous message. I splashed aftershave on my cheeks and chest, put on a dressing gown, turned off the bathroom light.

She did not move when I opened the door. A dim light

was glowing at the window; she seemed to be sleeping, but I was not sure. I had mentally rehearsed it time and again on the way home and felt excitement within my body at the prospect every time. So it did not seem unfamiliar when I walked over to her bed and pulled the covers halfway from her. She could not have been asleep, because she did not flinch when I touched the covers, merely turned slightly and looked at me. Her eyes glittered in the scant light, brown and clear. I could read nothing in them.

My dressing gown dropped to the floor as I lay down on top of her. She said nothing; her thighs opened as if she had known what was ordained and had nothing to fear. Her skin was soft and her hair too, her body firm but not too hard. I lifted her nightgown up to her waist, moved closer and . . .

Nothing.

My concentration gone, my nerves slack, my body unable to obey, I began to perspire with shame, lay still and sweated. It was then that she touched me. She stroked my cheek as she would a child; I felt the tenderness emanating from her palm. Like a child. I began to cry and wept for a long time, my face buried in her pillow. She went on stroking me but said nothing. That silent dignity. . . .

It must have been the wine. I have no other explanation. The next thing I knew, I woke up in her bed the next morning. That was the only time I have spent the night there. She had already got up, and brought me breakfast in bed as usual.

She did not mention what had happened the previous night and has never mentioned it since. It was as if nothing had happened.

I waited. The streets were empty. Those buildings once housed the Danish Royal Trading Monopoly for Iceland, chambers where men of means strode about in blue silk gowns, smoking tobacco in porcelain pipes. I needed to put all thoughts of those times out of my mind, could afford no distractions. I had to concentrate.

The passage through the warehouse led into an open yard. I stood a few feet inside the passage so that I could look out onto the street without getting any wetter than I already was. For the first time, I noticed that my feet were soaking wet. I heard a clap of thunder; the torrent was furious.

He came from a direction other than the one I had anticipated. Failing to notice me, he scouted his surroundings, looked down along the wharf, momentarily watched the boats and the rain merging into the sea. He turned a full circle, looked at his watch, pulled his overcoat up to cover his head. I called out to him. He did not see me immediately but ran to me when he saw me.

"Have you been waiting long?" he said.

I gestured to him to join me in the yard.

"What a downpour," he said. "I feel like a drowned rat."

"No one will see us here," I said.

"No one ever comes to this place. Why did you want us to meet here?"

"Did you tell anyone you were going to meet me?"

"Of course not."

That same officious air. That same braggadocio. All your vanity. . . .

"How long have you been with her?"

"What?"

"Don't pretend you don't know what I'm talking about."

"I thought we came here to talk about the movement. I didn't need to come here to talk to you about women."

"You'll talk about what I want you to."

I put my hand in my pocket and pulled out the pistol.

"Are you mad? What's wrong with you? I thought we . . . ?"

"Shut up. How long have you been with her?"

I pointed the gun at him. Self-confidence had vanished from his voice. He was shaking.

"Gudrún? Is that who you mean?"

I did not reply.

"A few months. I don't remember exactly. Why are you asking about her? What's she got to do with anything?"

"Are you pretending you don't know?"

"What?"

"We came here together. I came here to be with her."

"I don't know about that. She never told me anything. You must believe me. . . . I'm telling the truth . . . she never mentioned you. Not a single word. I'd never have. . . ."

He continued. Could not stop. Repeating the same

words and sentences, over and again. Trying to stop me from doing what I had to. Had to go on talking. Had to talk me out of it.

"What do you do with her?"

"What do you mean?"

"What do you do with her when she comes to see you at night? What do the two of you do?"

"Nothing. We're just friends. She comes to see me . . . sometimes she misses the train home. . . ."

"Tell me! I've followed her back to your place. I've stood outside in the street and looked up at your window when she's with you. Tell me!"

He had started to weep. The hero of the liberation was blubbering like a baby.

"You mustn't . . . please . . . I haven't done anything. I didn't know about you. . . ."

"Speak."

"Please . . . don't. . . ."

"Kneel down and tell me. Get on your knees and tell me!"

"Please. . . ."

He kneeled.

"Put your hands behind your head."

Unable to say a word, he cried like a baby, could not keep quiet, went on and on.

"Close your eyes and think about what you do with her. Think about it. When she's with you. Alone with you. Think about it."

I walked toward him slowly, walked toward his puffy face and his sobbing, his blubbering. The shot rang out clear and loud. The echo vanished in the rain. He slumped forward on his face into the puddle, jerked in spasms like a fish on a hook, landed on his right cheek, his left eye staring at me.

I woke with a start, drenched in sweat. So vivid. I could even feel my right index finger trembling and the pressure against it as I had pulled the trigger in my dream. When I sat up in bed, I realized I was holding the lamp from the bedside table in my right hand, had knocked off the shade and torn the plug out of the wall. Grasping it tightly, pointing it away from me like a firearm.

I got up. My bedclothes were wet, and the sweat was pouring down my cheeks and chest and stomach. I did not feel bad; no, I felt good, as after a long bout of sex. I feared that sense of comfort, even though it was not without pain, feared the trembling in my body and my yearning for more. Feared my thoughts. Feared much, that dark night.

What is she after? It is not money, nor marriage, nor passion. I don't know what her motivation is, for she never asks for anything, demands nothing, never complains. She lives from one day to the next and never mentions what will one day come to pass, does not say, "What will become of me when you die?"

Once when I was in a bad state (I seem to recall having been on new drugs that did not agree with me), I interrogated her. We had gone out to the Park and were sitting on a bench beneath the trees whose tops arch over the sidewalk on Fifth Avenue. It was evening. The streetlights went on while we were sitting on the bench. Generally, this is a moment of delight and tranquillity, but on that occasion my discomfort remained. The girl had arranged this walk, claiming it would do me good to move around and take in some fresh air. But I was dizzy and there was a foul taste in my mouth, my legs would not move as I wanted them to and my body was listless.

"What is it you want, anyway?"

"What?"

"I've been wondering what you're after. Don't imagine for a second that you'll come into all my money when I'm dead. I have many people to provide for."

"Those drugs are making you feel bad. Shouldn't we take a cab home?"

"I hope you're not plotting something behind my back. No one has ever succeeded at that."

"Let's go home. I'll cook you some soup."

"No one."

"Then we'll watch a good movie. Which one should I rent?"

I might have been somewhat indiscreet with her, that I cannot deny. The explanation is that I do not understand her, besides which the drugs were having a bad effect on me. I have always needed to be on my guard when dealing with people; it is a long time now since I learned to expect the worst. There are plenty of people who have tried to cheat me. I have often been stabbed in the back by people I would never have suspected of anything but the kindest of intentions toward me. I have long since ceased to feel upset by that, and have no other rule than to repay the misdeed many times over. Otherwise I would lose out. There is no point in telling someone who carves another person up with a knife, "Don't do it again, there's a good fellow." You have to chop off his hands to make sure he will not try again.

Since then I have never even thought of asking her why she is still living with me. I avoid mentioning anything that might raise that question. I am not sure I could take it if she left.

Before I depart, I shall prove to her that it was the drink that ruined my chances the last time. I shall show her I am no basket case. Then she will marvel at my power and stamina. I envisage her trembling with pleasure when I stand up afterward and open the window to let in some fresh air. She will fall asleep and dream beautiful dreams: green fields and a blue sky. And a chestnut horse in the field.

When I am gone, she will remember my lovemaking, her pleasure and the dream. That is how I want her to remember me.

Friends disappear and all others too, everything changes, nothing remains the same. How well I remember those days, the beginning and the end, every single minute as if in a flash before my eyes. Nothing can be retracted, nothing will be changed—a moment's rage, misguided vengeance, regret, flight. Regret: the world flares up and the searchlight swings above our heads. Yet still it is calm. I know: dust to dust, ashes to ashes, but the spirit—where does that go? The fingers holding the pen, the fingers I watch becoming immobile, disjointed, whiter. Do not incinerate me and do not put me in a coffin beneath the weight of the world, whence no one will return and whose walls are endless in all directions. Don't. In that dark hole beneath the weight of the earth. . . . For I fear death, I am afraid of the end, the nothingness and perplexity.

So much could have turned out differently. Providence, people say, instead of looking within themselves. I have seen people come and go, doors open and close; I know the moment of departure is invariably difficult. People wait for the lights to go on in the Park before they enter. They also wait for the footbridges to be lit up across the Hudson, where I sometimes used to go with my son Helgi when he was a child. People sit on the benches there or stand against the rails, staring out at the river and waiting for the lights to be turned on. Yet how paltry! What is there to marvel at? I would stroke my son's palm with my thumb, and he would say, "Dad, look at the lights!"

That is the way it has always been: light brings joy, but darkness instills fear. When I was young, I enjoyed nights most, but with age twilight became coziest. Now I want light and sunshine, darkness vanquished. How the mind changes. . . .

Helgi phoned the evening before last and I gestured to the girl not to put the receiver down because I wanted to talk to him.

"I just wanted to know how you were, Dad."

"I'm old."

"That's not the way you usually talk."

"I'm remembering old times, which suggests I'm old."

"It's been a long time since we've seen each other. You wouldn't want to come around for dinner, would you?"

I said I was feeling a little under the weather, and we should wait and see if I perked up in the next couple of days.

"Thanks all the same."

"We'd like you to come. I'd like that. For the children's sake. . . ."

For the children's sake—he had an intuition that the time was drawing near. Had his wife told him there was not much time left, and their children really didn't know their grandfather? I admit I was touched by his phone call, but all the same I disliked the tone of his voice. It was funereal.

"Did your sister ask you to phone me?"

"No, Dad."

"Are you sure?"

"Dad, please don't start. . . ."

"I was just thinking about when I used to take you up the Hudson. Do you remember that?"

"How old was I?"

"You would have been four. Four, five."

"No, I don't remember."

"Oh well. I was just thinking about it."

Silence.

"Maybe you'll feel better tomorrow. Should I phone then?"

"Maybe I'll perk up, who knows?"

"I'll phone tomorrow then."

"Give my regards to your wife. And the children."

He's really not so bad deep down, but lacks a cutting edge. Determination, toughness, initiative. He takes after his mother's side of the family. I am starting to believe that he is indifferent toward the inheritance. I am certain that money has no influence on his actions. It is his sister who is conniving. There is more to her than meets the eye. And that husband of hers: that good-for-nothing who sowed his wild oats all over the place until he married her, he's nothing more than her lackey now. She makes him stay home with their children in the evenings when she goes out. Turns him into a baby-sitter while she does as she pleases. A weakling.

I do not have the time to rail at them now, neither time nor energy.

The days are growing shorter; it is still raining outside my window. Last night the images haunted me again. When I close my eyes tonight, I know they will return: an eye staring up out of a deep socket, despondency and pain, the body nothing but skin and bones. I have seen those images in newspapers and books, on television and movie screens. Night after night those images flicker before my eyes, one after another: bodies like garbage in ditches and pits; I hear my name being called; the face in the vision changes. It is no longer from a newspaper or a book, but . . . no, I cannot bring myself to . . .

> There was frost outside. Four of us had been ordered to put on light blue overalls. The overalls were a new invention. Calculations had shown they were supposed to keep you warm in heavy frost, as long as you kept moving. We were the guinea pigs. There was the smell of new cotton when we put them on. Outside, it was sixteen degrees below zero. We walked around in circles. With poor footwear. I remember seeing them watching us through the window. They were drinking coffee. The mugs were steaming. When we fell down, we were kicked back onto our feet. They made us go on for seven hours. Two of us fell with an hour to go. They let them lie there to find out if the overalls were warm enough to keep them alive. I do not know what became of them. . . .

For years I avoided reading about those times and pretended they were none of my business. I erased them from my mind as a child uses an eraser to correct a spelling mistake. But gradually I gave way; before I knew it, that age of terror had gained a grip—or should I call it a stranglehold?—on all my thoughts. I amassed books and documentaries, papers and magazines, everything I could find, everything. Why did I not leave it alone? Why torture myself?

Never look back. Never think about what has already come to pass. But now I no longer know what troubles me more: recollection of the past or certainty about the future. I grow uneasier with every passing day, because I have much to complete before my turn comes.

I ask for peace. I shall give anything for peace. Silence and gentle sounds, the scent of a mown field, a wet trout in my hand. Have mercy, extinguish the smoldering in my soul: I cannot bear its burning of my sick body. I kneel before you, kneel in absolute humility: absolve me from my past, absolve me from my memories, grant me peace to prepare for my departure. The candle is burning, the flame slender and weak.

When the train left, I walked across the tracks and headed down the slope in the direction of the village. I passed a red-painted windmill before I found the main street and the boardinghouse where I had booked a room. There were few people about on the street, since it was only just past eight; I had taken the first train that morning, wanting to have everything set up by the time you arrived at ten. I thought the woman at the reception desk gave me a suspicious look, but that was probably just my imagination. I paid for the room; it would not be ready until two, she said. I told her I was in no hurry, since I intended to go for a long hike anyway before I returned.

A black mutt followed me up the street; I had noticed it outside the boardinghouse when I arrived. The woman had told me there was a café farther up the street, on the far corner facing the church. The mutt stayed behind when I went in. I could not tell whether this was because it was well trained or because it disliked the smell inside: a mixture of the aroma of coffee and the bitter stench of bad wine from bottles left open too long. Two soldiers were sitting at a table by the window, drinking beer; one of them looked in my direction, then continued drinking without saying a word. The proprietor was standing behind the counter. I sat facing him, drank black coffee and ate egg on toast.

"You come from the city?"

"Yes."

"Any news from there?"

"Nothing new. Same as usual."

He shot a glance in the soldiers' direction. "I need them here about as much as I need a kick in the balls."

I nodded.

"They can't understand a word. No need to worry."

"How many of them are here?"

"Too many. No news from the city?"

I shook my head and repeated that everything was the same as usual.

"Want a schnapps?"

"It's a bit early."

"Are you sure?"

"Maybe later when I come back."

"I'll spot you a schnapps then. When you come back."

The soldiers continued staring out the window at the empty street, drinking slowly.

"Where are you from?"

"Iceland."

"You've got the British there. You're lucky."

"I expect we are."

"Anything's better than these bastards. Hanging around here stretching out the same beer for hours."

I stood up. It was time to go meet you at the station.

"I'll spot you a schnapps when you come back."

When I walked out into the street, the mutt was gone.

It was four o'clock when we returned from our hike. We were comfortably tired, not too weary, after spending a long time sitting by a little waterfall beneath the yellow treetops, eating the picnic lunch I had prepared that morning when I woke up. Through the open doors of the church, the sounds of an organ could be heard: otherwise it was silent.

"Let's go to the café," I said. "The bartender said he'll spot me a drink."

"When does the train leave?"

"Half past five."

"Are you sure?"

"I asked when I arrived this morning."

"Is there one after that?"

"No. The next isn't until tomorrow morning."

There were more people in the café than there had been that morning: all dressed up, perhaps coming from church. No soldiers.

The proprietor smiled when we walked in. "Found some company, I see."

I introduced you to each other. You greeted him.

"I promised you a drink, didn't I?"

"I'll pay for it. And a coffee and a slice of cake for her."

"The drink is on me. I'll let you pay for the rest though."

I thanked him.

"Would the young lady like a schnapps too?"

You turned the offer down politely.

I disapproved of the way he looked at you, but still I felt proud to be with you.

"Any regrets about coming?" I asked.

"No, why?"

"It wasn't easy to persuade you to come."

"I wasn't sure I could get the time off."

"You played hard to get."

You smiled. "Wasn't it worth it?"

"It should have been."

What did I mean by that? You seemed uncertain of what I was thinking. Perhaps for the first time ever.

"Aren't you sure?"

"I was joking. More coffee?"

"What time is it?" you asked yourself, looking at your watch. "Five. When do we need to leave?"

"The station is only a few minutes from here. We have plenty of time."

Five o'clock: on target.

"Is the cake all right?"

"Delicious. Want to try it?"

"No thanks."

"She likes the cake," I told the proprietor.

"I baked it myself."

"You?"

He nodded. "But of course."

"Why are you being this way, Pete?"

"You're imagining things," I said.

Her cup was empty.

"Would you like another?"

"No thanks, we need to get moving if we're going to catch the train."

"What train? To Copenhagen? It left at five," the proprietor said.

You panicked. "What? Five o'clock? That can't be. You said it left at half past, Pete."

"No, the last train from Copenhagen gets in at half past five."

"What is its destination?" I asked.

"Jutland. Doesn't go back to the city until tomorrow morning."

"Pete, you said it didn't leave until half past five."

"The man told me it left at half past five. Who knows, he could be wrong. Let's go check at the station."

But the proprietor saved me the journey. "Hey, can you believe it?" he said to an elderly couple at a table near ours. "Somebody told him the train to the city leaves at half past five!"

"People nowadays."

"What should we do, Pete? What can we do?"

"Is there a boardinghouse in town?" I asked the proprietor.

"There's one farther down the street. But I doubt if you'll find a room; the Germans are there. Officers or whatever they call themselves."

"I must find a telephone. I have to let them know I won't be coming home. What will they say?"

I had no idea; I asked the proprietor where you could find a phone.

"At the boardinghouse. They'll be able to help you place a call there."

We walked down the street. The afternoon sunshine played across the roofs and through the foliage. There was a young man at the reception desk. The woman who had been there that morning was nowhere to be seen. He led you to a back room where you could phone. Meanwhile, I collected the room key.

"What did they say?" I asked when you reappeared.

"It could have been worse. Did you get a room?"

"We're in luck. There are only five rooms in the place. We got the last vacant one."

Silence.

"I'll sleep on the floor. They promised me an extra mattress."

"I suppose things could have turned out much worse."

"I suppose so, but we're laughing, aren't we?"

I sat on a bench outside in the garden and read a paper while you took a bath. When you finished, I would go upstairs for a wash. Two Germans walked by. "*Guten Abend*," one of them said.

"*Guten Abend*," I replied.

The couple sitting on a bench farther into the garden stared at me when the Germans disappeared inside the house.

Dusk was falling when we went out to get a bite to eat. You said nothing: your thoughts were elsewhere. The darkness settled over the flatness like a tablecloth over a table.

"There's nothing going on in this place," you said.

The church bell rang eight as we entered the café. A pleasant smell of food greeted us.

"Is this the only place to eat?"

"We should be grateful for whatever we can get, the way things have turned out."

"I can't understand how you managed to confuse the train times."

There was no mistaking it: you would have preferred to be somewhere else.

"You'll feel better after you have eaten something," I said.

The food was plain but tasty: chicken with gravy and vegetables. We drank beer from mugs.

"Make the most of it while you have the chance," the proprietor said. "The Krauts usually start rolling in after half past nine. I'm closing tonight before they come."

You cleaned your plate.

"Was it good?"

"Okay."

"You must have been hungry. Do you want another beer?"

"No thanks."

"Funny how we ended up here tonight. In this village, I mean. I didn't imagine we would be here more than a couple of hours. This is a perfect place for them to launch an attack. The Germans aren't prepared for anything."

"Perfect for who?"

"Our friends in the underground. You hang around with them sometimes, don't you? Jon and his pals. It would be interesting to hear how their campaign is going. This would be an ideal place for them to take the Germans by surprise. Maybe you should mention it to them."

"Why don't you?"

"I don't know them as well as you do. Sure you don't want another beer?"

"Positive."

"Some coffee?"

On the way to the boardinghouse the mutt I'd seen that morning appeared out of the dark and rubbed itself up against our legs. You were startled. I told you about our earlier encounter and stopped to give him a pat. "Good boy. . . ."

You were becoming impatient.

"Wouldn't you like to own a dog?" I asked.

"Come on. It's starting to get cold."

The sky was starry; I looked up and stretched.

"You're right. It's getting cold. It will probably be a chilly night. I hope the room's warm enough."

You gave me a quick glance, as if I had surprised you or you had suddenly realized something.

"Of course it'll be warm enough," I said. "We shouldn't worry about that."

My bed had been made on the floor and the bedside lamp was on. We both stopped inside the door.

"Lovely curtains," I said. "I'll wait downstairs while you get ready for bed."

There was no one in the lobby; I opened the front door, crossed the street quietly and leaned against the wall on the other side. The room faced west on the upper floor, and I watched the light inside and the shadow play against the curtains. Felt your presence on the other side of the windowpane. You were alone. I lit a cigarette. Soon the light will go out in the window, I thought. But by then I shall be up there with you. I stubbed out my cigarette on the wall and dropped it.

You were under the covers when I opened the door.

"Are you tired?"

"Yes."

I undressed down to my underpants, hung my shirt on a coat hanger and folded my sweater and pants. Then I turned out the light and lay down on the mattress on the floor.

"Is your bed comfortable?" I asked.

"It's okay."

"Is the mattress too soft? Too hard?"

"It's okay."

"That's good. I hope you sleep well. Good night."

"Good night."

Quiet. I lay on my back listening to the silence. Occasionally it was broken by a creak indoors or footsteps in the street, low voices, a muffled cough. You did not fall asleep right away but were tossing and turning. I waited for you to be motionless.

You were still when I got up and walked across the cold floorboards to the bed. You did not flinch as I pulled back the covers and was about to lie by your side. It was only when I touched the mattress that you turned toward me in the darkness.

"What. . . ."

"It's only me."

"What are you doing?"

"It's freezing cold on the floor."

"There's no room. . . ."

"You won't even know I'm here. Go back to sleep."

Dazed, you turned your back to me. I pulled the covers over me; you radiated warmth. I lay still for a while, but an uncontrollable excitement began to course through my body. I snuggled up to you and put my arm over your shoulder. You rolled over onto your back, as if responding involuntarily. Before I knew it, I was on top of you; before I knew it, I was kissing your mouth and your cheeks and your throat and your shoulders.

"What are you doing?"

"Gudrún . . . I love you. . . ."

As I moved down your body, kissing you, you grabbed my hair.

"Are you mad? What do you suppose you're doing?"

"I love you. . . ."

"Cut it out!"

"It'll be just as you want it."

I kissed your breasts through the slip as excitement welled up inside me.

"Get away!"

"Come on."

"Get off me!"

You slapped my face. Hit me and scratched me, did not let up until you had thrown me off you and onto the floor. You were panting. I was exhausted.

"What do you suppose you were doing?"

"You scratched me."

"What do you think I am?"

"Ask Jon."

"What do you know . . . ? Who told you . . . what I choose to do is none of your business."

I went over to the window and looked outside.

"Have you been spying on me? Have you been following me around? There's something clearly wrong with you."

Instead of answering, I lay down on the mattress on the floor. You did not want me. You were repulsed by me. I could tell. Even when you stopped talking and tried again to fall asleep, I could hear it from the way you were breathing.

I stayed awake on the floor until morning. Toward dawn I decided to take revenge. Vengeance: salvation.

We took the first train out in the morning. We did not exchange a word on the way back to the city.

D o I hear my name being called? Or is it an echo? A dream? Peter Peterson, it was you. Do I hear something being said? Whispered? Or was I dreaming?

Those voices in my solitude: they are multiplying. Now I hear them by day and by night, but they are silent when the images flicker past my eyes, as if not to disturb the show.

It was you, Peter. I never even suspected it. No one knew. Not a soul. It never occurred to me that you could have done it. You must have hated them beyond words. There must have been something that drove you and blinded you to do what you did. It suddenly struck me the other day that it must have been you. And now you are probably regretting it, now that you've grown old and soft, your flesh falling from your bones, your limbs stiff, and then it happens, Peter, life is over. There is no way to change what has been written, to delete or add.

I woke to voices this morning, not knowing where I was. There was still dream residue in my head: I thought I was in bed beside you that night long ago, felt I could sense the warmth of your body before you turned against me. Sometimes on awakening I seem to feel my cheek burning from your scratch; time and again I have made my way to the bathroom and looked in the mirror to convince myself that it has been nothing more than a dream.

You cannot imagine how I felt after that night. For the first time it dawned on me that I meant nothing to you. I was nothing more than a pawn on your board, which you thought you were free to move back and forth as you pleased. When I got on top of you, I realized how repulsive I was to you. How could I have been such a dullard, ever imagined that you might be fond of me? That we could love each other and be happy together? What daring and impertinence! "What do you think I am?" you said. "What do you think I am?"

I knew what you were. And I also knew that I would teach you that you could not treat me like a dog. But could I do what was needed?

It did not take long until I could.

I avoided you after that and did not keep in touch with any other Icelanders there either. They never asked me to come along anyway. In fact, I knew that they had never wanted me around. But that is another story.

I knew on the train back to the city that you could not wait to tell him about our trip. Every detail—holding nothing back. He would tell his friends, word would get around, and in a few days everyone would know.

"Do you think it's true?"

"I don't believe it."

"Pétursson?"

"What did she do?"

"I always thought he was weird. Don't you remember my saying so?"

"But not like that."

"So it must be true."

"Why would she make it up?"

"Bizarre."

"Keep your distance, girls. Don't find yourself alone with him."

I could hear them chatting away, sometimes whispering, sometimes excited, astonished, animated. She would ruin my reputation, if she had not done so already. I had to get away; there was nothing left for me in Copenhagen. Life was over for me there.

How well it could have all turned out if you had not turned against me. Our stay in Denmark and all the years afterward: endless celebration. I would have done anything for you. At the slightest hint of a wish on your part, I would have waded swamps to make it happen. You needed only to whisper it to me while I slept. You do not know what you lost.

We did not speak to each other afterward, and I left much more quickly than I had expected. I had always vaguely intended to go back home if I could find passage on a ship, but I did not want to leave you, and I had also given up hope that normal transport would be restored between Iceland and Denmark anytime soon. The passenger ship *Gullfoss* had docked in Copenhagen at the beginning of April and was impounded there after the German occupation. The Icelanders in the city, both those who were living there already and others who had been on the ship and were stranded, appeared to have nothing else to occupy them all summer but to try to secure passage home. I had nothing to do with them, I had other matters to attend to. It was not until my money began to run out that I understood the need to get away.

Money! Was it really money that changed my plans? As much as I might deny it outright, I know my children would not believe me. Certainly not my daughter. I remember the first time I heard her and her brother talking about me. She was barely in her teens. They thought I was asleep, when I had come home after a long drinking bout and gone to bed. The door to my room was shut; they talked in low voices, so I missed a lot of what was said.

"Infatuation with money, Mom," said Gudrún. "Sheer greed. He doesn't care about us in the least. Don't you realize that? Are you blind?"

I could not hear what my wife said in reply, but her sister who was visiting with us said something to the effect that she did not approve of the way young people today listened to screaming music and said nasty things about their parents.

"But you don't know him. You don't know what he's like. Mean . . . those eyes of his. When he takes offense. . . . Don't you ever get scared, Mom? Are you telling me that he never threatens you?"

"You ought to be ashamed of yourself," their mother said without conviction. "I don't want to hear that sort of thing."

"What do you think, Helgi?" his sister asked. "Am I not right?"

I could not hear what he said even after I got out of bed to put my ear to the door. Later I regretted not having opened the door a crack, for Helgi's words were the only thing that mattered to me. I pondered his reply, pondered it time and again. Years later I asked him about it but he pretended he didn't know what I was talking about.

"It was twenty years ago, Dad. Are you sure you didn't dream it?"

Was it money, though? I don't deny I've always felt an affection for money. Without it I am insecure; it gives me power and independence, for I do not seek luxury. It enables me to amass more wealth, greater power, and I fear relinquishing it, even a small amount of it. For then my power would diminish, I would lose more money in consequence, and more power, and so on and so forth until nothing was left. Would they be happy then? If I was left penniless and they did not know where the next cent was coming from?

I recount this only to prevent anyone from suggesting that I do not realize my own infatuation with money over these decades. But this was not true until you were out of my life. Money meant nothing to me when we were in Denmark. You were the one who drove me out of the country. It was you who forced me to commit my little crime.

I can never forgive you for that.

Hjalmur B. H. Storvik, a merchant and a friend of my parents, seemed unfazed by the long, tough summer. He had arrived on the *Gullfoss* on business, intending to spend a week in Copenhagen while the ship was docked there, but had been stranded after the occupation like everyone else. He had phoned me three or four times during the summer to suggest that we should meet, and I had always sidestepped the invitation. But when he contacted me in early September, two days after you attacked me, with some news, I decided to arrange to meet him. I could tell from the sound of his voice that he had not yet heard about what happened that night and I was surprised, because the Icelanders in the city were a closely knit group. It won't take long before he hears the story, I told myself, because she will never keep it a secret. If not today, then tomorrow. If not tomorrow, then the day after.

We met outside Frederiksberg Park, entering it on the north side through the main gate. It had rained the night before; the air was clear.

"It looks as if we'll be allowed to go home at the end of the month, my boy."

"On the *Gullfoss*?"

"No, first we'll probably have to take the train to north

Finland and a ship home from there. Petsamo is the name of the town. In the far north of Lappland."

"Really?" I said.

"The only sensible thing for you to do is come with us."

I kicked a pebble in front of me, two or three yards away, but did not reply.

"There's no sense in staying here. You'll run out of money soon, if you haven't already."

"I have more than enough for the time being."

"Then you ought to use it to get yourself back home."

The ducks were swimming in the canal alongside the walkway. I kicked a stone into the canal, and it sank with a plop.

"When are you leaving?"

"The twenty-fifth. We're going to Stockholm first and then north by train."

"The twenty-fifth. That's a Wednesday."

He looked at me with surprise. "What difference does it make what day it is?"

"None at all."

"You don't look well. Have you been ill lately?"

"It's just a cold. It's nothing."

"You look after yourself now. It'll be a tough journey."

Two young women passed us by. Hjalmur stopped to ogle them.

"*Oo-la-la, ma chérie!* I'll miss the Danish dolls. They've been the only bright spot all summer. The only light in the darkness, if you'll forgive the turn of phrase."

He was pensive for a moment, then seemed to realize something that had been on his mind.

"You haven't got yourself a Danish girl, have you, Pete?

That wouldn't be why you don't seem excited about going back home?"

He knew nothing about what had happened the other night. I felt relieved at his inquiry and smiled as I shook my head.

"When on the twenty-fifth?"

"What?"

"What time of day are we leaving?"

"In the morning. Early in the morning."

I laughed to myself. My plan was complete. Hjalmur B. H. Storvik had added the final touches to my scheme. The departure date could not have been better timed.

"I'll come," I said. "Count me in."

He looked more cheerful. "Good boy. Your parents will be pleased to see you."

We strolled out through the west gate of the park, out to Magstraede and down Gammel Kongensvej toward the Town Hall Square.

"This calls for a drink," Hjalmur said. "I wish I could invite you over to the Vivex so we could sit on the platform in the main hall and watch the band across the dance floor. But I haven't received any more money from home than anyone else. We'll go there the next time we're here. Whenever that might be."

"How much is the fare to Petsamo?" I asked.

"A hundred and twenty-five Danish kroner. I hope you can manage that."

"I can manage that and still have some left to buy us a drink."

"I won't hear of you paying. This one's on me, even if it costs me my last coin. No arguments, please."

"We'll see about that."

"Out of the question."

We strolled leisurely around the streets for a while; Hjalmur talked about what had changed and what had remained the same, pointed out store windows or signs on houses and said, "Just the way it was when I was last here."

What changes and what remains the same, what is transformed without our noticing and what vanishes without our remembering it ever existed. Changes, revolutions, and I knew that much would change over the next few days, in my life and others'. Instinctively, I clenched my fist and felt the strength in my fingers, the power, knew that nothing could stop me.

We went to one bar after the next, and the following day I woke up with a headache and an upset stomach; no chance that day would prove productive.

Helgi phoned me this morning and invited me around for supper. I put down the photograph of you that I have kept in the same place in my desk drawer for half a century and became pensive.

"Helgi, my son . . . ," I started, then stopped as I recalled what his sister had once said, something I was not supposed to hear but did: "Of course he'll accept an invitation to supper. He needs to eat like everybody else and a free meal saves him money. It won't take him long to figure out that the cab fare there and back is less than the price of some food and wine. Especially if the wine is good."

Time is short and there is no guarantee I will remember the events as clearly tomorrow as I do today. No guarantee I will remember anything tomorrow. It is impossible for me to count on being granted another day.

"Thanks, Helgi, it's a nice thought but I'm afraid I can't make it. There's a particular piece of business I have to finish. While I remember and have the energy. Will there be many guests? Just me. I'll send you a good bottle of red to have with the meal. Would you like that? I'll send you a bottle of Lafite '63. Wouldn't you like that?"

"Bring it when you can come. We'll try you again later in the week."

"I could send it over by car . . ."

"That's unnecessary, Dad. Bring it with you later in the week."

I must try to arrange the events mentally in the right order before I refill my fountain pen. The phone call disturbed my thoughts, but I did enjoy hearing his voice.

I did not know what I was letting myself in for when I told Hjalmur B. H. Storvik that I would join the group returning to Iceland. I am not referring to the ubiquitous hazards that everyone encounters in wartime (I faced up to them like everyone else on the trip), but to the fact that I could trust no one on the way. What if my little crime was discovered after we had left Denmark? What if it was traced from Copenhagen to Stockholm or from Stockholm to Petsamo or Petsamo to Iceland? Every moment of the way I was expecting to be fingered. I thought I could see accusation in the eyes of my traveling companions: sometimes I felt they moved aside only to whisper to each other: It's him . . . we got a telegram from Copenhagen . . . it's him. On constant alert, even though I had no escape route. Nights and days while we rattled along in the train, while traveling in darkness, or in a fresh morning. On constant alert, prepared for the worst, by myself, alone, with no hope of support.

That experience would have toughened up my son. Remorse would have strengthened his inner self, solitude would have boosted his self-confidence, the journey would have taught him vigilance and patience. He has never been in peril, never had to wrestle with difficult questions. Life and death, anger and forgiveness, punishment and suffering. Never.

I need the strength of a distant summer while I commit

those days to paper; I need beauty to be able to recount the ugliness, happiness to remember the sadness. I put the cap back on the fountain pen and head off to the wine cellar. The girl has gone out. I open a bottle from a distant summer. The wine gives off a scent of berries and heather. And its color is charming in the light. Beauty pleases me, but all the same instills melancholy and regret. This is the way it always is when I sip old wine.

We were setting off at eight o'clock the following morning. That was when we were supposed to meet down at Havnegade 49. I was hoping that we would not stay there long, I wanted to get away before anyone began to suspect me.

It was four o'clock and the autumn sun was shining outside. Fall is like a middleman you cannot trust: warm as summer at first, then cool and windy before finally yielding to winter. Perhaps that was why I had begun to notice distrust in people's behavior over the past few days.

I had packed my luggage in two suitcases, which were waiting by the front door. I needed only them and an old trunk to accommodate all my belongings. The trunk was still in my room, crammed with books and various little oddities I had collected. I had settled my account with the old lady that morning; she was not pleased that I was leaving, said it would be difficult to find as easygoing a lodger as I had been. "And I always liked your girlfriend too." I tried to smile when she mentioned you.

For the umpteenth time I went over the plan in my mind. Had I forgotten anything? I had the note in an envelope in my jacket pocket; I had typed his name and address on a typewriter at college; it would be impossible to trace it back to me if it fell into the wrong hands. I had arranged with a neighbor to take me down to the harbor the following morning, an old man who owned a horse and cart. He was going to come by at half past seven.

The sun was setting. I went to the window to watch the sunshine fading on the roofs in the quarter. I suspected this was the last time I would ever watch the sunset in Denmark. I would not miss the country. The butcher down the street came out onto the sidewalk and lit a cigar, looking lazily about: time to shut up shop and head home. Calm. But there was an uneasiness too, a premonition of mental struggles and sleepless nights. Too late to call it off now. No reason to call it off now.

Around dinnertime Hjalmur phoned.

"Finished packing?"

"Yes."

"We're going out to a restaurant on Kongens Nytorv. Me and two or three other Icelanders. How about coming to feed your face with us, if you'll forgive the turn of phrase?"

"I don't think so. I need to say goodbye to my friends before I leave."

"Then we'll see you at eight tomorrow morning. Make sure you don't oversleep, old boy."

I did not feel like eating. I had to get going if I wanted to make it to the gathering by half past eight. I opened the wardrobe and made sure the letter was in the pocket of my jacket. A white envelope. I held it up to the light, then put it back in my pocket.

It was dusk when I went out. King Christian's birthday would be two days from now and the storekeepers had decorated their windows with the Danish flag and photographs of the king and the royal family. I walked past the stores without stopping, noticing the pictures out of the corner of my eye but lacking any inclination to take a closer look. I quickened my pace: What if he gets there early and leaves when he doesn't see me? What if I miss him tonight? But he definitely said he would come tonight, yet things can always change. What if he doesn't come? I had broken into a run before I realized it; it was twenty past eight and there was no guarantee that he had the whole evening to himself, even though I had told him I urgently had to see him that night.

King Christian was also in the windows of the B. Andersen & Sons bookstore. By himself in one window, in the bosom of his family in the other. I stopped outside to catch my breath, pretending to be contemplating the window displays, and having done so, I darted inside.

Andreas Klotz was not there. A low lectern had been set up in the customary place: the reading would soon begin. Some people had taken their seats, others were browsing through books on the shelves and on the tables. A young woman sat down on a chair in front of the lectern, took a violin from a case and tuned it. She was supposed to give a recital before and after the reading. I sat in the back row, next to the door. She began with a theme I did not recognize, and her playing did not calm me: why is he not here? A man in front of me put his arm around the shoulder of the woman by his side; she leaned her head toward him. Vivaldi, Bach or Schubert. I became increasingly uneasy. Something must have happened. Andreas Klotz was usually so punctual. I did not recall his ever being late before, except once. What if he doesn't come tonight? I had to leave the next morning. I could not. . . .

I did not notice him until he was sitting by my side.

"I got held up," he whispered. "Have I missed anything?"

"She's just started," I said.

"Schubert."

The audience applauded when she finished. She stood
up and bowed shyly, but instead of walking away, sat down
again and put her violin back under her chin. She's playing
some more, I said to myself. Long and lethargic notes followed, suspended in the silence. I grew restless. My companion seemed to notice.

Eventually, she finished, and left by a back door. I was
getting ready for the break, fishing in my jacket pocket to
check if the envelope was still there. But the break was put
off and the reading began without an intermission. It was a
quarter past nine. In less than eleven hours I would be
down at the harbor with my luggage in two suitcases and a
trunk, and the crime behind me.

Danish translations of German poetry. The translator
read the original before reading his rendition. I had long
ceased to pay attention. But there was no mistaking that
Andreas Klotz was having a marvelous time.

Applause. I braced myself in the chair. A short break,
ladies and gentlemen, coffee and cakes on sale at the usual
place, a few signed copies of the translations available at the
cash register. The envelope was still in my pocket.

The guests stood up and spread through the store.
Most of them queued in front of the refreshment table;
others leaned against bookcases or doorposts for small talk.
The handful of signed copies seemed to be selling well.
People I had seen there before greeted me. I returned their
greetings, even though I would have preferred not to rec-

ognize anyone there that evening. A good thing no Icelanders frequented the place.

"She didn't play too badly," Andreas Klotz said.

"Who didn't?"

"The girl. Schubert. She didn't play too badly."

"No," I said. "She played well."

He reached into his coat for a pack of cigarettes.

"I'm going outside for a smoke."

We went out and lit up outside the window where King Christian was by himself. There was a friendly calm about the people in the store, but I was beginning to panic.

"Are you cold?"

I inhaled the smoke and nodded. "I'm leaving tomorrow."

"Where to?"

"Iceland. Via Sweden and Finland. The Icelanders here have been granted free passage by the British and the Germans."

"I suppose it's just as well for you, the way things are. There's no telling how long it might drag on."

I stamped out my cigarette. I must do it now. If I don't, nothing will come of my plans. Now. Must do it now.

"I have something for you," I heard myself saying as I watched the cigarette butt I was still stamping out.

He did not reply.

"Let's move away from the window," I said.

We walked up the street. The light from the store window soon waned. Shadows on the corner.

"What's this all about?" he asked, putting a fresh cigarette in his mouth.

I felt inside my jacket pocket and handed him the envelope.

"He's in the resistance," I said. "His name's in the envelope. Address too."

He glanced at me, then at the envelope.

"Why?"

I had not expected this question, but replied unhesitatingly: "He's compromising others. He's dangerous. He influences people. He . . ."

I stopped. He put the envelope in his pocket.

"I have to leave," I said.

He shook my hand. "Bon voyage."

"Wait until I've left before you do anything," I said.

"I'll wait."

Instead of letting go of his hand, I pumped it again.

"I'm going now."

"Maybe we'll meet up again. Bon voyage, Pétur."

I walked away. Slipped my hands into my pockets, zipped my parka up to my neck, and walked away. He was still standing there on the corner watching me the last time I looked back. I could see the glow of his cigarette and feel his eyes following me long after I was out of his sight.

The evening was cool and bright, the stars were glittering, but I could not see the moon. I did not look to my right, or to my left; shadows flickered on walls and lights shone in windows. I quickened my pace, a villain leaving the scene of his crime.

n this occasion we remember the days when every-
O thing was carefree. Our thoughts turn to quiet
mornings beneath the trees heavy with leaf; a book in our
hands, crowds milling in the park. We remember how surprised we were at everything when we first arrived here.
But a new age is upon us, a more tragic age. People move
nervously, as if they know they will have to flee for shelter.
We bid farewell to this country and this nation that has
treated us both well and badly, has been our adversary and
companion for centuries. May the Lord God Almighty
protect them. We pray for our fellow countrymen who are
staying behind and say to them: may life smile upon you."

Almost nine o'clock. The organizer of the journey was
standing on a soapbox. I hoped his monologue would soon
come to an end. There were cheers of hurrah for King
Christian X; a Danish student was making ready to deliver
a message from her nation to the people of Iceland, a
young blond woman.

Would we ever get moving? I was restless: the endless
farewells, good wishes and hugs. I could not see you, there
were so many people on the quayside.

"Pétur!"

I flinched.

"I haven't seen you since last year, when you'd just arrived."

"Kristjan," I said, but could not remember his last name, having met him only two or three times the previous fall.

"So you're going back home too."

I nodded, but before I could utter a word in reply, he started talking to someone else.

I noticed you when the passengers began boarding. You were by yourself, standing in the middle of the crowd. As far as I could see, you were greeting a couple I seemed to recall having seen at some Icelandic gathering in the city. Your hair was blown across your face by the slow morning breeze; you brushed the locks away from your forehead and arranged them with the fingers of your right hand. I stopped by the gangway and let others pass ahead of me so that I could watch you. You had not changed: your smile was warm, your cheeks rosy. Yet I thought I could detect a hint of sadness in your smile. What had I done to you? A sudden pain in my stomach and chest and head. What had I done? I stared at you, could not tear my eyes off you. What forces were tugging at me? What charm? Your soft hair, your petite fingers, your breathing when you slept by my side. What could I do now to be able to hear that again? Every night until I die. Anything you want, everything.

I shook my head. Wishful thinking, I said to myself. It is over. I knew I was looking at you for the last time. My little crime behind me and no one I could trust. You scratched my face, I thought, and involuntarily put a hand to my cheek. Why did it have to turn out like this?

"Scared?" I heard a voice behind me ask.

Hjalmur B. H. Storvik placed a heavy hand on my shoulder. "Everyone's scared, Pétur old boy. Everyone's scared."

There was a faint smell of alcohol on his breath.

"We all have to stand together. I volunteered to lead the group that will be staying at the Hotel Regina in Stockholm. I've been there before. A first-rate hotel, Pétur. We ought to be in good hands there. I had some merry nights there once, if you'll forgive the turn of phrase."

He went on board. I looked around for you, but the crowd wandered off and I could not find you. I wanted to see you once more, just once. I walked away from the ship and into the throng: people were saying their farewells and embracing; uncertainty in the air and a suspicion that this was a turning point in their lives. I could not see you anywhere. Could you have left so soon? While the ship was still docked? Suddenly, I caught sight of you as the crowd reconfigured. It was as if the waters were parting between us. Our eyes met. I did not know whether for you this was good or bad. My mind was vacant. We stood for what seemed like an eternity. When I sensed you were about to take a step in my direction, I turned around and rushed up the gangway without looking back.

I'll wait," he had said, but there was a strange timbre in his voice. What if he waited only a day or two?

The trip by boat to Malmö was as uneventful as the train journey from there on to Stockholm. I did everything I could to avoid the other passengers, nodding or shaking my head when addressed, saying little. Fine weather for the whole journey, and on the train to Stockholm, people started singing. In no mood for jollity, I kept to myself.

What if he is arrested before we get back to Iceland? You would put two and two together, make a few inquiries, discover that I had gotten to know Andreas Klotz in the bookstore: you would know that I informed on him. A message would be sent to the leader of my new companions: there is a criminal in your midst, Pétur Pétursson. "I'll wait," he had said, but his voice was strange and his expression enigmatic. Could I trust him?

There was no hint of a world war in Stockholm. There were no indications on the streets when we arrived at our hotel close to midnight: only fit young athletic men, some in shirtsleeves with sweaters draped over their shoulders; young women in beautiful coats. My thoughts were wandering uncontrollably.

"There's a fuel shortage in the city," I heard someone say.

"Fuel shortage! If that's all there is. . . ."

The party split up. Some went to the Park Hotel, others to the Hotel Alexandria, still others to the Hotel Continental. There were other hotels too, whose names escape me. Instead of undressing after going to my room, I stretched out fully clothed on the bed, the lights off, my eyes open. I had not been lying there long when there was a knock on the door. "It's me, Pétur."

I could tell from his voice that something had gone wrong. Had Andreas Klotz broken our agreement? Couldn't he have waited just sixteen hours?

Should I deny all of it? Of course I would, but all the same I was in no mood for dissimulation, unable as I was to bring myself to say: "Me? How could you think such a thing of me? You can't be serious. . . . I don't know whether to laugh or be insulted."

In no mood for that, I opened the door. Hjalmur was panting, had clearly been running from one room to the next.

"Things look bad, Pétur. Bad."

I asked him in, but he stayed in the doorway. Was he afraid of me?

"Bad news. The Germans intercepted the ship that was to meet us in Petsamo and they forced it to go to Trondheim."

I felt relieved at first and had to take care not to show my delight, until I realized that I was in more trouble than before: every delay invited peril.

"How long will it be in Trondheim?"

"No one knows. We have no choice but to wait."

Long days in Stockholm. I spent all of Thursday and Friday lying in bed, neither reading nor sleeping, staring at the ceiling and out the window. I thought of your face in the crowd. Why did I turn my back on you?

On Saturday morning I took a walk in the drizzle and grayness, went to a bookstore, trying to put everything out of my mind. Hjalmur made an attempt to get me to accompany him and others to a restaurant, but that was hopeless. I had no longing for human contact. Long and gloomy days; the memory of them saddens me.

On Sunday a telegram arrived from the captain of our ship. They had left port in Trondheim that morning and expected to dock in Petsamo on Wednesday.

"No sense trying to leave here until the ship reaches its destination," Hjalmur said.

"Madness," the organizer said. "Nowhere to stay on the way."

We waited. Monday passed, and Tuesday—days of absolute inactivity. On Wednesday afternoon we set off on a northbound train for Finland. I avoided conversation, since that might well have prompted questions I did not want to answer. The train passed through valleys and forests with fading autumn foliage, past glittering lakes and the impressive houses of wealthy farmers, tidy villages and machine-gun bunkers on the hills along the tracks. Some of the girls began to give themselves airs and made a point of singing for the soldiers we passed. Their smiles would disappear from their faces if they knew of my little crime. I looked down the carriage in turn at each of my compatriots and confirmed what I had suspected: I could trust no one. I was on my own.

Where will they arrest him? On a train or at sea? Will I be back home then? What will I be doing at the moment when they knock on his door and say, "You're coming with us"? Will I be awake or sleeping? Laughing or brooding? Will I perhaps be on my way home from a dance, pleasantly tipsy after a little too much to drink? I did not know, and felt it was strange to think I could exert no sway over the matter.

My fellow countrymen ate ceaselessly. They began to think of lunch the moment their breakfast had disappeared down their gullets. That rapacious crowd who sang and made music as if nothing mattered but feeling good and filling their bellies: they bored me and I was unnerved by the prospect of not being able to get away from them in the weeks ahead. Cretins, I said to myself, damned cretins.

On the last leg of the journey from Tornea to Rovaniemi the train crawled more slowly than before, stopping frequently. This disturbed me until I found that they had only logs for fuel, beside which there was heavy traffic on the line. Gas lamps were lit in some of the carriages and candles in others. My fellow countrymen complained as the candles burned and demanded more on the spot. Brats are never satisfied. They began to disgust me. It would not take them long to turn against me if they heard about my little crime. No matter what I said, it would make no difference if I pleaded with them to believe me. People like that would be delighted to eviscerate me. You can bet on that.

"Come and join us in a song, Pétur! Chin up, nothing else will do!"

Intolerable rabble.

I prayed for rain, a fine shower in the still weather to calm my mind. The rattling bus on the bumpy road kept me awake. I had by now not had even a moment's sleep. The train had stopped in Rovaniemi; we were traveling the final three hundred miles to Petsamo on buses. Since there was no room for all of us inside, the younger and fitter members of the party sat up top with the baggage. I preferred that to sitting among that appalling crowd.

It was night when we set off, nothing but darkness and quiet. I prayed for rain. I had an intuition of sloping hills in the darkness, stunted woodland in the valleys and up the slopes where moss took over. If it rained, I would be able to smell the scent of birch. Perhaps I would hear a whimbrel chirping in the drizzle. I sensed that the birds in the woodland shied away as the buses drove past. Then everything fell silent. Noises, rumbling, the accelerator pressed and released by turns. Rattling in the dark of night in the far north of the land of autumn.

Everything would lighten up sometime. Like waking from a bad dream. I forgot what had happened and turned my thoughts toward what would be. I felt drowsy in the trunk, my head dropped. I was startled when the bus hit a bump. Soon day would break. A new day unlike all other days. Perhaps it would begin with a fine rain.

Go to sleep. Don't let me scare you. It's me, your grandpa: a monster in human guise. Come on, get to bed, it's late. You hardly know who I am and you know nothing of my past. Yet there is fear in your faces, hesitation in your eyes. You see nothing but an ailing body and the walking stick I left at the door. My fingers no longer move at my bidding and my legs sometimes seem to take on a life of their own. Do not judge me, though you fear me. I shall send you candy at Christmas, a big bag full of candy. There was a time when I could have played with you on my knees, but now it is too late.

The sun rises beyond the green hills and sets between the red trees in the clear autumn air. Sins are forgotten and errors are annulled as the years pass, but everything takes time and the human mind's capacity for remembrance is strong. A man walks with his son around the lake, strokes his palm with the thumb of his left hand and says: "It will start snowing soon. The lake will be frozen over." To those of you who are young and carefree, I say: It too shall pass. The ice will melt on the lake, the footprints will vanish from the snow, hands will build houses and houses will be razed. It too shall pass. Perhaps you will remain alive in the memories of other people, but they too will disappear and it will be as if you have never existed.

Why am I thinking that, why on earth, while you sit there facing me, well behaved, wearing lovely clothes with your hair well groomed? Why am I not thinking about the wine that Helgi is pouring into the glasses and the turkey that my daughter-in-law is carving so deftly? Her movements are wonderful. Why don't I say: "What a delicious turkey. I don't recall ever tasting such fine poultry. And the wine, Helgi, you couldn't have made a more harmonious choice. Coochy-coochy-coo. Not shy of your old grandpa, are you? Do you want gramps to play a game with you afterward? Tag? Hide-and-seek? Or a game of cards?"

But my appetite is dull and I can scarcely taste the wine, even though I have often drunk it before and know it is delicious and would cheer the heart. I take a mouthful of turkey that I've dipped in sauce and sweet potatoes, but do not enjoy eating, do not enjoy anything, feel I am out of my body. Where does the soul go? Nowhere. I know that.

The girl greets me when I return home. She and Helgi exchange greetings; I cannot detect any ill will between them. Good, I think, I am too weary to engineer a reconciliation. Good.

"Were you bored, Dad?"

The girl helps me take my coat off, takes my scarf and hat; I sit down on a chair in the hallway and take my shoes off.

"My mind was wandering, Helgi. I don't feel too well. I'm old. But don't for a second think that I was bored. Far from it. Let's get together again soon."

"Cathy was pleased that you came. She's always thought you didn't like her."

"Tell her I was touched by the invitation. Tell her I told

you that I'm not sure you deserve a woman like her. Go on, tell her that. Of course, I don't mean a word of it, but women like flattery. Vanity, Helgi. It has a grip on every one of us."

A smile of surprise and unexpected joy, yet unease in his expression.

"I'll phone you tomorrow."

I nod and stand up.

"Early afternoon."

I pat him on the shoulder.

"Good night, Dad."

I wish him good night and sit in the parlor. So his sister has failed to poison his thoughts. He has not turned against me as she has; after all, he has disliked squabbling since childhood. "Don't argue," he used to say if I happened to raise my voice at his mother or sister. "Please, don't argue."

I wonder what his brother is like. The boy whose paternity Hannes had assumed. I wonder if there is a resemblance to Helgi? Too late to think about that now, far too late. I have plenty to occupy me, need to turn my thoughts to what remains unresolved.

I intend to leave everything in order behind me. Maybe I shall do something for Helgi.

Britain? Why were we going to Britain? And we thought we would be back home in Iceland on Thursday. We woke up on that gray Tuesday morning of October 8 and saw that our ship was sailing south.

We were only 360 nautical miles from Jan Mayen yesterday, sailing west, north of the island. Thursday, we'd been saying. We would be back home by Thursday. Our nerves taut. I went up on deck and lit another cigarette. The sky was gray and overcast, the waves pounding against the hull and a knot in my stomach. I stroked my cheek; it was four days since I had had a shave.

The previous afternoon I had entertained high hopes of being out of danger. I even went to the evening get-together and listened (without feeling sick) to the passengers singing and the readings from newspapers that they had arranged since Sunday. I also watched a magic and dance act and was beginning to think it was about time to shave.

Britain. The trip upset me from the start. When we sailed out of Petsamo Fjord on Sunday, I had spent a long time looking toward land (the factories, jetties and oil tanks), watched the children playing on the slope overlooking the town and knew that our passage would not be as peaceful as their games. Just before sunset the coastlines of Finland, Norway and Russia came into sight. On the edge of the world, I thought, far away from everything and yet still not safe.

Why? people were asking. No answer. Why don't the British simply inspect our cargo and documents once we are back in Iceland? What were we going to do in Britain? It must be because of me, I told myself: they must have uncovered my villainy. But . . . how? They must have. Why else would we be going to Britain? Silent disquisitions, uncertainty, fear. Was anyone eyeing me suspiciously? The captain had not done so when I bumped into him that morning. Perhaps he did not want to give the game away until the British had arrested me. Another cigarette. Yet another cigarette to twiddle between my thumb and index finger. Another day, another night; mile after mile in a gale and in fear.

P eterson?"
   "Yes."

He looked at the passport, then at me.

"Peterson. Not too tough a name to pronounce compared with . . ."

No one had paid attention to us when we reached Orkney on Thursday evening and cast anchor in the Papa Sound. Warships and planes were nowhere to be seen that day, nor the day after, when we sailed in bright breezy weather to Kirkwall.

"They have their reasons," Hjalmur B. H. Storvik said with a knowing expression. "They have their principles. We have to follow the same rules as everybody else."

"Couldn't they have waited until we got back to Iceland?"

"Principles," Hjalmur said. "Principles are principles in war. That's just the way it is."

Perhaps they were going to arrest me without creating a commotion. Scrutinize all the passports, so it wouldn't look as if they had gone straight for me without a thorough inspection of everyone. *Festina lente.* Take all the time you need. I shall not be going anywhere. Don't hurry yourselves. I was not surprised when I heard that they were going to leave the luggage alone. There was nothing to find there.

"Took a quick glance at the passport," Hjalmur said, "but left my bags alone. Routine. Nothing but routine procedure."

Of course they did not care about the luggage. It was the passengers that they were interested in. They were inching closer toward me: Saturday afternoon and they were still nosing through the others' documents.

"It's good to be able to rest here in the harbor," Hjalmur said. "I'd had my fill of those rolling waves. When are you going to shave, my boy?"

Five o'clock. Three minutes to five when they came to me. I handed my passport to them. Both of average height, one pale and stocky, the other swarthy and thin. The latter spoke for them both.

"Peter Peterson."

"Pétur. Pétur Pétursson."

He tried to repeat my pronunciation, but had trouble making the liquid é sound.

"Peterson. Not such a tough name to pronounce compared with the others."

I nodded.

"Going home?"

"Yes."

"Been in Denmark long?"

"Just over a year."

"What can you tell us about the Germans there?"

Instead of answering immediately, I lit a cigarette. Offered each one, but they both refused.

"They're everywhere," I said. "They've taken over the

hotels and boardinghouses, restaurants and pubs. But it's all very peaceful, because there's no resistance."

"Did you get to know any of them?"

"Why would I want to mix with them?"

They took another look at the passport.

"I knew there was something. I couldn't quite put my finger on it at first, but now I realize."

He stared me in the face. If I was not mistaken, the pale one shifted his weight onto his other leg, as if preparing to pounce. So this was it.

"What's wrong?" I asked.

"That stubble," he said, smiling. "You haven't shaved for a while."

I rubbed my chin.

"That's what's funny about the photo in your passport."

Could it be true—had I escaped? I kept a low profile for the rest of that day, played chess with Hjalmur in his room, four games with cigarettes for stakes. Just before dinner, when the British had gone, I accepted a glass of cognac from him. Not swallowing it at once, I let it rinse my mouth, nip my tongue and palate before allowing it to ease down my throat. I could feel the tension draining out of my body.

I took care to conceal my joy, but as a little treat for myself I allowed Hjalmur a checkmate in the last game.

The moon riding the clouds. Glaciers ahead in the shimmering moonlight. Although most of the passengers had retired to bed, some were still up. We would be arriving home the next morning.

Home: grass rustled by a gentle breeze, a shower of rain shattering the mirror of the lake. Would anyone have fallen asleep tonight with a Tarzan comic book in his hands, a little boy with his head full of dreams? The autumn air as clear as glass. When I inhaled it on the deck, I felt an inexplicable reverence for creation. For Iceland. Yet I would have to leave there again. Forsake it.

No need to think about this. Allow me to enjoy the glaciers in the moonlight and the temporary peace visited upon me. I knew that it would vanish again, so allow me to enjoy it for a few moments more.

It did not vanish the following morning when we anchored in the outer harbor in Reykjavik, even when armed British soldiers boarded the ship. I relished looking at the mountains around us and the buildings in the city, the smell of fish and seaweed and the canvas stretched over the goods in the sheds by the harbor. I kept my calm all day, even when the British were brash and rude, interrogating all the passengers and demanding from each of us the names of six good citizens who could attest to our characters. I feared nothing, because the abuse was directed at all of us. They were not after me. Knew nothing. Not a damn thing.

Mother and Father greeted me when I disembarked that afternoon. I hugged them and for the first time in a very long time felt affection for them. We held hands walking up the wharf to Father's car, and I resolved to forget the past.

An old man's memories haunt him every day. Nothing ends until the eyes cease to see and the fingers to move, not until the heart ceases to pump blood to the brain. Then, at last. . . . Errors and failings are never forgotten. Attacks on me are preserved in my memory. Should I envy my cohorts who have lost half their brains and entered their second childhood? They do not wake up at night from nightmares, but smile at trifles and sleep like infants when dusk descends.

People who spend their old age at peace with themselves and others do not notice that the world has become a dwelling place for clowns and drummers, that the end is drawing near and our capacity for change dwindles with each passing day. Hustlers lie in ambush for us. There are traps by the wayside. But you do not notice them, you say, "Everything is the way it was, the sun comes up and the sun goes down to rest." Your bellies full and spirits softened by a moment's fun. The Lord speaks out for the wretched, you think, stands up for righteous weaklings. Those who have been awake need sleep. Others go on sleeping.

Every spring for the past few years a bird has laid eggs in a window box on the ledge outside my bedroom. I do not commit this to writing for any special reason; no, it only entered my mind when I looked out the window. Because it is cold now and the straws in the window box are being wafted by a chill breeze. People driving alongside the river early in the morning see the smoke from the furnace more clearly in the frost. They see it before the first rays of sunshine light up the eastern sky and know it will merge into the brightness of morning when the streetlights are turned off. People who drive alongside the river early in the morning on their way to the airport know what I mean. People who are leaving have seen the smoke on the far bank of the river. The rest of us, we remain behind, go nowhere. We suspect that our next journey will be longer than all others.

A woman phoned the night before last when I was at Helgi's. A foreigner, the girl said. She said she would phone back, but before hanging up she asked my address. Surely it couldn't have been my niece, I thought. She must be pushing fifty now. No, it can't have been her. I have never heard from her, do not really know her at all.

It might have been a journalist. They have tried to get hold of me in the past. An Icelander abroad, they say. People back home want to read about Icelanders who have been successful abroad. In America. Of course I have always refused to meet with these people and told them to keep their prying noses out of other people's business. But I would not be surprised if it was a woman journalist giving herself airs.

"Young?" I asked the girl.

"No, elderly."

"And did she leave her name?"

"No, she said she'd phone back."

The girl finally yielded last night and bought herself a new dress. I had been trying to persuade her for months, but in vain until now. Yesterday I threatened to go to the store myself if she would not.

"You're not up to it."

"I will all the same."

She went.

I sat down on a chair in her bedroom while she tried on the dress. I enjoyed watching her take off her sweater and pants, fold the sweater and place it on the bed. She did not seem disturbed by my watching her put on her nylon stockings and petticoat; her breasts are white, and her thighs slender but beautifully shaped. If only I were younger! If only I had the strength! Those little breasts, shaped like pears. Her hair black and soft and nice to run your fingers through. Power in my body, an unexpected force, and I would take her in my arms, help her out of her petticoat, lay her down on her back. Her pears would be delicious and her petite hands would guide me. If only I were younger. . . .

She put on the dress and black shoes. Around her neck she put on the white pearl necklace I gave her last year. Twirled around in front of me. Smiled.

"Well?"

Thanksgiving next week: stuffed turkey, cranberry sauce, sweet potatoes. A glass of wine.

"Well?"

It looks cold outside. I want to spend my last days with her.

C hristmas.
I have always looked forward to that season, looked forward to the lights and warmth and reverence for an imagined divinity. For as long as I can remember my eagerness has not diminished with the years. That is why I am disturbed: the lights have been on in the parlor and study since Thanksgiving, but they have kindled no joy in my heart. I have tried everything: turned them off for a day or two in the hope that I would start to miss them, yet I feel the same. As to why this should be, I have no explanation.

The turkey that we ate on Thanksgiving was tasteless. I could hardly detect the sweetness of the potatoes. The wine brought me no pleasure. Is the end near? I asked myself. A journey into the depths of silence and the unknown? The girl urged me on: "You must eat some more," she said. "Are you unwell? You've hardly touched your wine."

Now she is out buying Christmas presents for my grandchildren. Something nice, something of quality, I told her. She wore her new dress at Thanksgiving and looked more beautiful than I could ever have imagined. She sat beside me when it was time for dessert and let me slip my hand under her dress; she did not complain when I rubbed the part where her stockings and flesh met.

At this time of year the days are short in Iceland, and in New York it grows dark early too. Silence indoors, bustling outside. I sit in the green chair in the study; tourists take horse-and-carriage rides through the Park: thirty dollars for a half hour, if I recall correctly. They look forward to promenading along the streets afterward, admiring the decorations in the store windows and the rows of lights and holly strung between the buildings and across the streets. Lovers go to cafés, pleasantly tired after their Christmas shopping, compare notes and drink hot toddy or tea or a drop of whiskey with their coffee to warm their bodies and their hearts. Guests sitting at the bar on the south end of the Park see the horses bow their heads and rest between rides.

I turn the letter opener around in my hands. It would have been cleaner to drive a knife through his heart. You . . . no, I shall leave that unsaid. Everything comes to an end, memories disappear, and before I know it everything will be as if I had never existed.

A snowfall was forecast on the television last night. Calm weather, a snowfall and a light frost. When I peeped through the curtains, it was still clear, but the sky had a snowy look about it, as gray as the street below where people were clambering out of yellow taxicabs with their bags and parcels. The bells on the Christmas lanterns tinkled when I let go of the curtains: a picture of a log cabin on one of them, a snowman on another, children in a chair in a warm kitchen on a third, a burning stove beside them. I vividly remember buying that decoration. It was a few days before Christmas—Helgi was with me, he could not have been more than six. "Won't you buy it, Dad? Please." Would he remember that now?

When I was a boy, I used to spend Christmas Eve afternoon sitting by the parlor window, looking over toward the cathedral and waiting to hear the bells ring. "You always do that, Pete," my sister Disa would say. "You always wait there, even though you know the bells won't be rung until after five o'clock." Father would light a fire in the hearth after lunch and have a glass of port and cookies at three. At half past five we would set off for the cathedral, on foot because it was not far to walk. I used to think *Silent Night* was the most beautiful of all the carols. Maybe I'll get a new toboggan for Christmas, I remember thinking once on the way home after the service. Father was holding my hand, and I clearly remember wondering as we walked up to the side of the pond whether I would have a toboggan. A long time ago, but not really. Everyone is gone. As if it were yesterday. As if it never happened.

I hope the girl will find something nice for Helgi's children. Something of quality. I made it clear to her not to worry about the price. Perhaps she is still looking for presents for them. I hope she does not buy anything for me. I always forbid her to do so.

On Christmas Eve I shall take a bath at five o'clock as I always do, then dress in a dark blue suit, put on a deep red tie and place a handkerchief in the breast pocket of my jacket. There will be an aroma of cooking from the kitchen when I emerge with my cheeks tingling pleasantly from aftershave. I shall open the wine around midday to allow it to breathe, then go to the cellar to look at my bottles. You will be wearing the black dress that I bought for you, with the white necklace. I shall be aware of your presence in the kitchen without seeing you, hear your footsteps and the tune you hum softly over your work.

That is the way I wish to remember you, when I disappear into abysmal solitude, into a darkness unimaginably black, into a light brighter than the sun. I wish to disappear in peace and forget what was and what could have been, forget everything except you in your black dress with your white pearls, a coy smile on your lips.

This is the way I remember you in light and shade, in the modest silence after the thunder and rain.

*S*team rises from the streets after the rain. I have been sitting out on the balcony since noon, before the rain started, beneath the green canvas canopy she hung last spring. The balcony was one reason we rented this apartment. We lived together here for almost two years. Our separation was brisk and largely free of turmoil, on the surface at least. Then, emptiness.

The manuscript is lying on a round white table in front of me, beside the ashtray, a tobacco pouch and a lighter that is running out of fluid. An empty coffee cup in my hand, Beethoven's Seventh wafting from inside. I have been counting the tiles on the balcony floor and the cars driving along the street below.

It was almost morning when I finished working on the manuscript. Then I lay down to sleep and did not wake up until almost noon. I have not missed many days from work since I received the pile of papers from Schwartzman almost two months ago, which is why I have no qualms about taking today off. Admittedly, my thoughts have sometimes wandered at work, but that is hardly worth mentioning.

Pétur Pétursson died early in the spring. March 22, to be precise. I could not help wondering shortly after I had read his writings why he had stopped before Christmas and did not pick up his pen again for the final months of his life. The most obvious explanation would have been that he was too ill to do so, but Schwartzman dashed my theory when he told me that Pétur had *never been admitted to a hospital, but died at home in his sleep. Strange, I remember saying to myself.*

I lay awake at night composing theories as to why he stopped writing when he did. Once my colleagues caught me staring idly into space without my noticing them. There were times when I was in pretty bad shape after she left, and they might have assumed my state of mind had something to do with her. They said nothing.

Then came a point when I began to pry even further into Pétur Pétursson's private affairs. I had already gone too far (I was aware of that), but I still could not restrain myself. When I returned the manuscript to Schwartzman and told him there was nothing to be gained from it, I did not mention that I had made a photocopy. I regretted that for a moment, then forgot it. It could not have made any difference to him, I thought.

One Saturday morning, after much contemplation, I took a cab across the Park to Pétur Pétursson's home. I had phoned the previous evening and had not really expected anyone to answer, suspecting that the apartment would have been sold by then. I was surprised when she answered—"the girl," as he called her. I introduced myself as a compatriot of Pétur's and said I wanted to let her know what he had written about her in the manuscript. Would I be imposing? No, I could come by, she replied.

How small she looked in that huge hallway! A polished parquet floor, a mirror on the wall and a table beneath it, with a vase of flowers. At a glance, the hallway looked larger than my own sitting room. She invited me inside; I thought that she somehow clashed with the heavy furniture of the parlor, the dark wood paneling covering half the walls and the presence of death that I seemed to sense the moment I entered.

"The Christmas lights?"

"I took them down."

I asked whether I might take a peek at the wine cellar. She nodded, and I followed her through the hallway into a wing where the wine cellar was. I could tell that her bedroom was beside it, and that his was at the far end. Racks of wine, from floor to ceiling, a thousand bottles at the very least.

"Two thousand," she said.

I did not think it was proper to ask to see his bedroom, and she did not invite me either. We sat down in the parlor again. Finally, I explained my business to her, telling her I could not allay my suspicion that something must have happened which made him stop writing three months before his death. I knew it was none of my business, I said, but this suspicion was haunting me. She ought to know that he lavished praise on her in his memoirs, and I was prepared to translate selected passages for her if she was interested, I told her. She listened without saying a word, then said she did not know whether anything in particular happened. I asked more questions; she answered in monosyllables, shaking her head or shrugging.

Only after a long while, she told me about the visit. Two days before Christmas, on December 23, just after lunch. An old friend, the woman had told the doorman. He let her go up without phoning first to announce her arrival. The girl was not in when this happened; she had gone out shopping.

When she returned, she could not understand what they were saying because they spoke in Icelandic. But she could read his expression and later she would piece together the odd passing references he made. She told me what she knew (how hard it was to wheedle a complete sentence out of her!) and suggested I should talk to his son Helgi, who might know more.

"And you can always borrow the tapes, if you want."

"What tapes?" I asked.

She disappeared into his study and returned with an envelope containing some cassettes. Seven, to be exact. When I asked her about their relevance, she said that he had begun talking into a tape recorder when he stopped writing. A Dictaphone, she called it, and said she recognized it from when she was his secretary.

We shook hands in the hallway as I was leaving; I held her hand for a moment and told her how pleased I was that she would be able to stay in the apartment for another twenty years. I was not surprised at his designating his grandchildren as heirs, I said. And her.

Seven cassettes. It was not until I had listened to them time and again, memorizing every word and nuance of his voice, that I dared commit his account to writing. His voice disturbs me, wakes me at night, addresses me during the day when I least expect it. Please do not let him invade my mind, I pray to Almighty God. To what depths will I descend?

It has been a hot summer, and humid. When I awoke this morning, I stretched out toward her instinctively as if I did not realize that she is gone. Sometimes I think I can detect her scent on the pillow. I have still not been able to bring myself to put this pillowcase away in the cupboard.

Tonight I shall sit in the sitting room and listen to some music, in darkness, making do with the indirect street lighting through the balcony doors. Sometimes when it was too hot to sleep in the bedroom, we would move into the sitting room. Then we would open the balcony door and stretch out on the floor on our quilts. It was good to make love in the warm breeze from outside.

Everything was fine then. Tonight I shall listen to some music and fiddle with my pipe. My fingers are sore from typing. I have a hunch that fall will have arrived when I wake up tomorrow morning.

I have put my pen away in the drawer and the inkwell is gathering dust on the desk. What a waste of time, I say, what a waste of time, as I contemplate the people on the street on this cold winter day. Here, February is the coldest month.

In some ways dictation into a tape recorder is more efficient, but I do not look forward to hearing myself describe the event. When I write my reflections down on paper, I can sometimes persuade myself it is the pen that controls the account and I am merely acting in an advisory capacity. On the other hand, if I speak there is no question about who the author is.

I do not know which is more difficult to live with: guilt or deception. I was accustomed to the guilt; at least my crime was the cause of it. But deception—this is what others do to conspire in my humiliation.

I felt as though I had awakened from a dream when you stood in front of me. At first I did not know you, did not recognize you at all, was on the verge of slamming the door in your face and calling that kid doorman to ask him how you had gotten in. But then you opened your mouth: "Pétur, is that you? Is that you, Pétur?"

No! I said to myself. No, it can't be you. An old woman, grotesque with fat. I did not know you. And your hair was purple. Not dark and soft, but purple. How should I have reacted? You walked into the hallway, I helped you out of your fur coat and placed it on a chair, showed you into the parlor. I was weary, my fingers so numb I had to rub them together to revive the feeling in them. I heard you admiring the apartment, the paintings and the books, but it was as if your words were coming from afar.

"What a long time it's been," you said. "Half a century. I had to take you by surprise. That's why I asked the door-man to let me in. . . ."

I went into the kitchen and fetched you a glass of water, because I seemed to hear you saying you were thirsty. My legs were still unsteady and my ears were ringing, so I stayed by the sink and splashed my face with water. Where's the girl? I hoped she would get back soon. I had thought it was her.

"I arrived four days ago and looked you up in the telephone directory right away. When I couldn't find you there, I asked my son to find out your number at the bank. They seem to know everything at that bank. I came to visit him and his family. They've been living here since the fall and are staying until the spring. He's working on some project for the bank. Not that I can claim I'm really clear as to what he does. . . ."

I did not recognize the voice, but you went on chattering away. Your son was sent here from Denmark for a few months and this gave you an ideal opportunity to visit him. The grandchildren—you could not face being away from them for so long, had to see them, if only for Christmas and New Year's.

"The last time we saw each other was down at the harbor, when you were leaving Denmark. Do you remember?"

Objects were revolving before me, the paintings on the walls. The books, chairs and tables. I got up.

"I'll fetch some more water."

"We never said goodbye. For some reason or other, we never said goodbye. I think we've always had a soft spot for each other."

That crone! What was she rambling on about? She was not the tiniest bit like you. . . . How should I know this woman wasn't just impersonating you? You didn't bear the slightest resemblance to each other. A totally different voice. How should I know who she was?

"Those were some times we lived through. You should think yourselves lucky that you got back to Iceland safe and sound. I never dared to make the trip myself, as you remember. I was certain the Germans would sink the ship. . . ."

Rustling in the hallway, a door shutting: the girl was back home. She looked in; you got up and introduced yourself. You shook hands.

"Shall I make some coffee?" she asked.

I nodded.

"Or tea rather?"

You said you would prefer tea.

The girl disappeared into the kitchen; I could hear her fumbling with a kettle and cups.

"I never left," you said. "I was stranded there. Got married in '42. Maybe you've heard?"

I shook my head.

"But I probably didn't even meet my husband until

after you left. He was a medical student then. Henrik Avildsen. He died the summer before last. Oh dear. . . ."

Silence.

"But tell me about yourself. I've said more than enough."

She didn't seem to know anything, I said to myself. I had to say something to stop her from rambling on. I didn't want to hear her mention his name. Didn't want to hear her say, "You probably don't know what happened to Jon, do you?"

"I came here early in '41," I heard myself say. "I've been here ever since."

You asked me about my children. How many? And grandchildren? Aren't they wonderful? They light up your old age. You told me you have three children, if I heard you correctly. Grandchildren . . . I stopped listening, gave the occasional nod.

The girl brought tea and coffee and a plate of biscuits. I could see her reading my pained expression, but she still could not understand what was happening or do anything to help.

"Half a century, Pétur. I was beginning to think we'd never meet again. If Sven hadn't been sent here by the bank. . . . Have you kept in touch with any of the crowd we went around with when you were in Copenhagen?"

"No," I rushed to say before you started naming names. "I haven't seen or heard from anyone since I came here."

"Stina and Haukur took the ship back to Iceland. Almost all of them took the ship home. . . ."

I stood up, supporting myself against the back of a chair. Don't say any more! Spare me! I didn't want to hear his name. Two days before Christmas and you turn up here like it was yesterday. Unrecognizable, grotesque with fat and purple hair. Who sent you? Who is behind all this?

"Some water!" I call out to the girl. My hands begin to shake.

"Are you all right, Pétur? You don't look too good."

I don't? How do you think you look? The girl brought a glass of water. I drank it in one gulp and slumped back into my chair.

"I'll be here into the New Year. Maybe we can get together. Go to the theater or get a bite to eat. It's such a terribly long time since. . . ."

You were getting ready to leave, so I agreed to all your suggestions: we really must meet up between Christmas and New Year's, go out for a meal, to a concert or the theater. Really must do that.

The girl helped you put on your fur coat. You kissed me goodbye on the cheek. The appalling scent of perfumes and cosmetics.

"That reminds me," you said when I pressed the elevator button for you. "Jon sends his regards. I told him before I left that I was going to try to get hold of you. Send him my regards, he said. My very best regards. So now I have. He stayed behind, like me. We meet sometimes. His wife's Danish. A teacher, like him. Of course, they're retired now."

The elevator door opened.

"Well, old pal. Goodbye for now. And Merry Christmas. You have Sven's phone number, haven't you? We really must get together before I leave. Merry Christmas!"

The door closed and you were gone as suddenly as you had appeared. I supported myself against the doorframe, with both hands, and slumped to my knees. The strength had left my legs, darkness was before my eyes, and there was a ringing in my ears. Man is like a breeze, his days a fleeting shadow . . . she came to me, stroked my cheek and helped me to my feet. Deception. Pure and simple. All these years. I leaned against her for support; Christmas lights somewhere ahead of me in the darkness. When I stretched my hand toward them, I felt a sudden warmth against my body.

I shall depart for the abode of no man. You lead me through the dark, support me, stop me from falling. I want to be with you, alone with you. We grope our way toward more light.

Flowing light.

ÓLAFUR JÓHANN ÓLAFSSON was born in Reykjavík, Iceland. *Absolution* is his first novel to be published in English. He studied physics at Brandeis University, and is currently president of the Sony Electronic Publishing Company in New York City.